SELFIE AND C

SELFIE AND OTHER STORIES

Nora Nadjarian

ROMAN *Books*
www.romanbooks.co.uk

ISBN 978-93-83868-24-7

Typeset in Adobe Garamond Pro

First published in 2017

1 3 5 7 9 8 6 4 2

British Library Cataloguing in Publication Data
A catalogue record for this book is available from the British Library.

Publisher: Suman Chakraborty

ROMAN Books
Kemp House, 152 City Road,
London EC1V 2NX, UK
Unit 119 and 120, Park Plaza, Ground Floor, 71, Park Street, Kolkata 700016, WB, India
www.romanbooks.co.uk | www.romanbooks.co.uk

Printed and bound worldwide by
LSI and its partners

STRETTO

A FICTION SERIES

Series Editor: Jonathan Taylor

'... a plurality of independent and unmerged voices and consciousnesses.'

– Mikhail Bakhtin

Stretto is Italian for 'narrow' or 'close,' often used by musicians to refer to climactic sections of fugues where the voices overlap more closely, where the polyphonic texture is particularly intense. *Stretto* is now also a groundbreaking series of novels, novellas and short fictions, which takes on Mikhail Bakhtin's well-known conception of 'polyphonic' literature, intensifying it, playing with it, developing it in new contexts. Here are fictions which are multi-voiced, polyphonic, fugal in many different ways: fictions which are multi-perspectival; fictions which stage clashing, sometimes dissonant voices; fictions which hear from marginalised people; fictions which interweave human voices and musical voices; fictions which engage with voices from other places, other disciplines, other worlds. Above all, here are stories which are themselves musical, lyrical, dynamically contrapuntal.

Selfie and Other Stories by Nora Nadjarian is part of *Stretto* Fiction Series.

CONTENTS

SELFIE AND OTHER STORIES

EXHIBITION

Chairs hang from the ceiling. Do not touch. They move themselves, not all the time, not all at the same time. So it's a bizarre effect when a chair, a wardrobe, a bed, seemingly decides to express itself. They hang by invisible wires from the beams and have pencils attached. Their motions write indecipherable messages on blank sheets beneath them: meaningless, desperate, like a memory, or a child's attempt at an alphabet, all over the place. Each one seems to have something to say: the longer you look at it, the more meaningful, the more insistent, the more enigmatic.

The one that spoke to me was the piano stool, the round, wooden, swirling one. I had not seen one of those since the days I used to sit next to my piano teacher, the formidably Russian Miss Nina. A red velvet cushion was placed under my little bottom to make me taller, my small fingers concentrated on Brahms' Waltz in G-sharp Minor and Nina repeated, *More! More open! More open! You are playing closed! You are playing like a cage!*

When she left me to have a pee, always a few minutes before the end of the lesson, I would swirl a full 360 degrees on the stool until she came back. I tried to play "more open" in the last five minutes just to please her, whatever playing open meant. I wanted to play round and round, open and opener, sharper and Majorer, but it all came out sad, flat, G, Flat, Minor.

And the trace made, on the white sheet, is a circle of lines that criss and cross as the stool spins and my little feet swing in and out.

The exhibition space is like a stage. *I would like to thank... I'd like to thank...* And the artist's tongue is tied, she can't remember who. The only person who comes to her mind is her father who used to pack and unpack his suitcase, all on the same day, without travelling anywhere. He would put all his clothes in, and the pipe, and the tobacco. Then he'd lock the suitcase and carry it all the way down the stairs, only to carry it back up again, into

11

the bedroom, onto the bed. And open it. It was a ritual that reminded her that her father was alive, that he was there. She often wanted to slip a message into the suitcase when he wasn't looking: Dad, I love you. Or: You have no idea how much I'll miss you. Or: Please don't go.

The spotlight faces her like a full moon. It blinds her. And they all applaud because her exhibition has reminded them of things about their life that they had long forgotten. The piano stool, the table, the gramophone, the suitcase – all part of the past hanging from the ceiling into the present.

Somebody hugs her. It's her father, dead now for almost four years. He tells her he has read the notes, that it finally now all makes some sense to him. *Thank you*, he says, *I packed my whole life into that suitcase, and there is no longer any need to unpack. I'm home. Finally, I'm home.*

The exhibition space is one street away from The Street of the Whores. The whore is cooking a stew with bay leaves, stirring in other spices from her rack, at random. The front door is open and the place smells divine. Any passer-by would be tempted. Soon, there is a cockroach scratching its legs behind the gas cooker and there is a man sprawled on the sofa, wearing shorts and a stained singlet, and she is saying *I'm coming, I'm coming.* They are a romantic couple, the whore, her client. Even a ménage à trois, if you count the cockroach.

She closes the door and starts taking off her clothes. A big, fat lump of nothing, that's what she knows she is. Her feet almost shuffle as she walks towards him in the dim pink light. She wants to tell him something indecipherable, something meaningless, something desperate about her life. But this is business, and business is business.

The whore's mother insisted on her death bed that she had three daughters, not four. *No, no, the third one died when she was very young, I only have three daughters*, she declared. Her eldest daughter, the one with the perfectly shaped eyebrows, sat on a wobbly chair by her side, held her hand all the time.

A long time ago the whore was a girl. *You can come and kiss me on a first come first served basis*, said the girl with fuchsia breath and she smiled like the bold-coloured flower that she was. She breathed onto their faces, watched them turn pink, red, fuchsia, fire, free.

There is always a beginning, and in the beginning, she sold kisses by the hour. Men came, men went. Gradually, slowly, time passed, life passed, they did strange things to her lips, mouth, nose, ears, hair, skin, turned her body inside out, outside in, smiled, swore, broke her, unbroke her, touched her, undressed her, dressed her, told her stories, bought her, sold her.

She is now a ghost of her former self in the dim pink light. She writes her autobiography in her head. The words are all there, the questions, too. *Tell me, did you once love me? No, I mean really love me. Tell me, did you think of me as a woman or as a whore? Do you still dream of me in fuchsia dreams, the girl I was, the girl I became? If you saw me now in the street, would you recognise me?*

She thinks of the man, sometimes. The man without a name. The man she loved. She loved him, but he insisted on paying her. He loved her, but wouldn't leave his wife for her. Long, long, long ago.

After the exhibition, the restaurant is full of literati and glitterati sipping chilled white wine. Snippets of conversation collide in the air. *Yes – absolutely incredible – I simply – did you? – purest materials – They couldn't possibly have – No, of course not – the raw one…*

A mobile phone rings. The zip of an enormous handbag opens, zzzzzzzzzip, and then closes again, zzzzzzzzzip, somebody talks to the phone and to the party at the same time, a pregnant woman coughs, a glass of water is knocked over.

It is mid-summer and there is a slight breeze. The candle on the table is blown out, the waiter reappears, apologises, strikes a match, lights the candle, and retires again into the shadow, somewhere to the left of the palm tree. *The baby moved*, the pregnant woman whispers to her husband. *He moved*, she whispers again, and holds his hand.

The morning she finds out she's pregnant, the woman looks at the sky and smiles. It looks almost painted, she thinks. It could have been painted this morning. In nine months' time she will give birth to a son. He will be the most beautiful creature her eyes have ever seen.

But for now she admires the sky. It reminds her of a mural she once saw in Florence. She looks for the photo of the mural but she can't find it. She can never find the photo she wants, in the same way she can

13

never think of the right word to complete a sentence. Instead, in an envelope in one of the drawers of her desk, behind a pile of old letters, she finds five photos. Five photos of her and her husband and a blue sky above their heads. Behind each of the photos, her small, neat handwriting says: Italy, 2005. Behind the sky, she thinks, is a date I had forgotten. On the other side of the sky is a date.

She is not in Italy but the sky is so blue. The sky is so blue, almost a blessing. Five photos of a blue sky, they lift her spirits. She lays them on the table in front of her, plays around with the order, arranges and re-arranges her own private exhibition. She takes a deep breath, takes in the past, lets it meet her future.

The baby will grow up to become a man. But for now it is a foetus in the dark. His bones are still soft and pliable, he has not yet been fully formed but his life has started. His mother tells him his life has started, that he will have black hair like his father, that she has given him her green eyes.

There is a sunny spot in the garden, and this is where she stops, like a satisfied tourist, and talks to her unborn son about things he should know about herself and his father. Because we might change, she says, as you grow older. One day we will be different people, we may not even recognise ourselves in the mirror. One day, we may not be able to recognise you. So I want to tell you all this now. I love your father and he loves me. I love you as much as I love the blue, cloudless sky.

The baby moves slightly, it is as slight a movement as the blink of an eye, but enough for her to know that he's listening. *We made you*, she whispers to him, *a long time ago. You were born many years ago, in Italy.*

Days later the artist thinks there is something wrong with her, the way she sees the world all askew, the way she can't balance her feet when she's walking. Like a bird, she can't keep still on the ground. It's almost as if the road she's walking on doesn't exist anymore. But it was here yesterday, she mutters, to no one but herself. But I was here yesterday. Step by step, she thinks she is escaping reality. Her life is a figment of her imagination, playing tricks on her mind. Whenever she passes by a mirror she smoothes the worry lines, she smiles, tries to remember her face when it was younger.

On difficult, unbalanced days, she photographs graffiti or takes found objects home and polishes them like there's no tomorrow. Once she found a pebble. A pin. Part of a sponge, a shell, a broken light bulb, a shoelace, a receipt. She wanted to record the sound a pebble might make under her foot as it clicks against another. She wanted to make an asymmetrical sculpture, one that would inspire longing in people. The feeling of longing, the sensation that only those who have lost something would know about. *Excuse me, have you lost something?*

She wonders how long the road is back to her childhood. *But you can't go back*, said her father, only forward. Yet she longs for something. *For what?* asks her father. *I just long for*, she replies. *It's a state of being, longing for. Something.*

The bird lands, and hops. She feels that she is hopping from one place to another in the same city, like a homeless person, a nestless bird. Her father visits her in dreams and tells her: *You're making an exhibition of yourself.* She wants to make sculptures out of things people have lost. *I've lost a pin, a pebble, a coin, an eyelash, my heart, my mind. What are you longing for? What have you lost? When did you last see your heart? Did you pack the suitcase yourself? Please do not leave baggage unattended.* People always want an answer to make them feel good, she thinks. And she knows that when there is no reply to a question, it is considered an asymmetry.

She thinks of her mother. They went to church every Sunday, she lit candles. But her mother was discovered one afternoon, when her husband came home early from work, went up the stairs and opened the door. The whole neighbourhood held its breath. So you've been married to a whore all these years, they didn't ask. So your daughter might not even be your own, so nothing you know is true, so somebody pulls a carpet from under your feet, and you lose your balance. Look out, you're about to fall. And her father lost everything he thought he had, securely, in his hands, his head, his past, his present. Start packing, follow her, change your mind, unpack. You're a loser, a fucking loser – your wife walked down some stairs and disappeared from your life. He sometimes wishes he'd come home early that night only to find that the lock on the door had been changed. Then everything would have been different. Then nothing would have happened.

The city hides its secrets. If you want to explore, walk in and out of the present, into the past, way back into the past, follow narrow paths and open doors to re-enter the present, to go round cement blocks, in and out of artificial lights.

I, the author of this story, am putting things in the right order or no order at all. I am trying to express in words how I was never able to play the piano openly. My playing was rigid, cemented. Nowadays I prefer to listen to CDs, and write. I am opening up in other ways, I suppose. I've found the key of the cage. I've discovered some words and I'm putting them together and I'm writing and writing.

The exhibition of the hanging chairs is still on. I went to see it again yesterday. There they were, all the seemingly random objects on seemingly random display, hanging from the ceiling. The whore's chair, the artist's father's suitcase, her mother's bed, Miss Nina's piano stool. I stood in the middle of it all, and I didn't know how long I spent listening to their stories, to the silence charged with their unearthly frequency.

Tonight there is a gecko on the wall, a tiny creature with tiny black eyes like beads, a transparent body. I want to keep it there for company, on my wall, forever, to illuminate it with a coloured light. But it moves away, runs away from me, hides somewhere in the dark.

Miss Nina plays a Nocturne by Chopin. I try to catch the music in my hands, I pretend to be playing it myself beautifully, faultlessly. I am seven years old. For once, Miss Nina does not speak. For once, I long for her to tell me off, to tell me I'm playing it all wrong. I long for her irritated voice, her Russian accent. But she says nothing at all. She turns the pages of the book and plays another Nocturne and then another. I swirl 360 degrees on the stool next to her and finally I lose her, she's gone. All I have is the music in my head. C. Sharp. Minor. There is no book, no piano, no room.

Things shift from here to there and from there to here. The ghosts of the old town write their diaries. Please don't touch the exhibits, they move on their own.

MRS GASLIGHT

For two weeks now, I've been trying to figure out if people are laughing with me or at me. I've been trying to push doubts as far back into my mind as possible. To smile at myself more, in the mirror. To remind myself that the woman smiling at me is really me. Maybe everything is her fault, after all, and not mine. Maybe I have changed into some other woman, someone I don't recognize. Just like he said last night: "I don't recognize you anymore. Why are you making life so difficult for everyone around you?"

One thing's certain in my mind. Things have changed, and in the last few weeks have become worse. I'm a character in a play, but I've forgotten my lines. I just keep apologizing all the time, that's all I seem capable of. Take last night, for example, I failed to cook that dinner in time. It was all my fault, and then our guests arrived, and the food was still uncooked in the oven and when Liz came in to ask if everything was all right, I just said yes, I'm sorry, yes, everything's fine, it's just that I was out walking the dog and lost track of time. It was true about the dog, but I also had this idea that I should impress him and our guests with a new recipe, something I found in Good Housekeeping. A Cajun Shrimp and Sausage gumbo.

A few days ago I asked him if he'd like to try something new, a new dish and he said Yes, about time too, I'm sure our guests will appreciate something different for a change. He finds me boring. I knew it right there and then, how could he not, with the way I dress and talk, and my complete lack of social skills, my quiet-as-a-mouse timidity. I wanted to impress him with this new recipe, but when I started off, it was all so confusing. I realised I'd left the green peppers at the check-out, and also discovered we were out of thyme, so I had to drive out again. I got the measurements wrong, I wondered if I'd put too many shrimps in, so it took some time to get started, and then before I knew it the guests were arriving. Liz walked into the kitchen wearing a beautiful black dress and looking glamorous with her hair tied up in a bun, all slick and shiny. She asked if everything was alright and I said Yes, thanks Liz, everything's fine. I managed a small laugh and added, Thought I'd try out this new recipe, that's all. She laughed too, but I was almost sure she was laughing at me.

I can't remember much about the dinner itself, except that Liz and John said it was delicious and Liz even asked for the recipe, though I'm sure that was just to make me feel better. He, I mean Dave, said the sausage was too heavy and that I should test new dishes out before inviting guests to be our guinea pigs and he looked at Liz and they both laughed. I know, I said, I'm sorry. And frantically searched for my next few lines, but as usual I couldn't remember them. Just that one word repeated over and over, again and again, in my head: No! No! No! No! I always try to push it as far back as possible, so no one will see it, so no one will know I'm disappointed. How can I keep doing this to him? How could I have humiliated him in front of Liz and John? When will I ever learn?

The last time my sister was visiting she asked me if I needed any help. I don't mean with the washing-up or cleaning or tidying or anything like that, she said. What then? I asked. I don't know she said, blushing, It's just... It's just that... I can't put my finger on it... I... but I'd stopped listening because my mind was struggling with that little word No, No, No, all over again. I made her a cup of tea and we talked about her children, and for once I was relieved that I didn't have to think of what to say, because she was doing most of the talking, and I even managed to smile, once or twice. Then she brought up Alan, and talked about him for what seemed to me an awfully long time, about how he helped her in the kitchen, how he never put her down in front of others, how much she trusted him to give her the right advice, how secure he made her feel. And then she said something which sounded so loud and so odd, it almost made me jump. You could leave him, she said. Leave. Your. Husband.

It was as if a jigsaw puzzle had gone all wrong. She had ruined a jigsaw puzzle which had been put together to form a perfect whole, a beautiful picture. And what was I supposed to say? She obviously has no idea how much I love my husband. I told her that. You have no idea how much I love my husband, I said. She just stared at me, and I wondered if it was the woman in the mirror she could see. Then I smiled, but she just looked down at her cup of tea.

Everybody's laughing at you, he said. Just pull yourself together. Don't you know what your sister meant? It's pretty obvious to me. She obviously meant if you don't know how to handle this marriage, you should just get out of it... And to be honest with you, I've had my doubts about it myself, lately.

The words started swimming in my head. My heart started pounding. I was looking once more for that dark place, any place, where I could curl up and sleep just for a while without anyone knocking at the door, banging at the door, wake up, wake up... I know they're all laughing at me. My sister, my family, my neighbours, my friends.

And you? I asked.

What?

Are you laughing at me, too?

Darling, just try to understand. I'm only doing what's best for you. I love you.

I...

I love you.

Yes. I'm sorry. I'm so sorry.

When he's working late at the office and I'm lying in bed, the lines come to me. What I should have said and forgot. Sometimes I imagine we're dancing, and there's no one else around, and I feel that warmth of happiness in my heart, the glow of love burning on my cheeks. On other nights, I remember an old boyfriend who asks me how I am, if I'm happy. Then there's a face looking at me, indistinct, like an enlarged photograph stuck to the wall, like wallpaper. I can't really tell who or what it is because I'm too close to it.

And then there are all the new recipes I've taken to memorizing, the shopping lists that go with them. Our next dinner party will be perfect, I feel sure of it.

19

BLUE PEAR

The air smells of damage.

The apple has a slight tinge of red on its skin. She has moved it, she has moved it to the edge of the table, somewhere. It's going to fall off the edge into the depths of nothingness. Green hides yellow, black. Colours shift, her kitchen has become a place for dizzy meals, her head hurts. She's going to fall. They do not really smell, these apples have no real scent. What she needs is the smell of pine trees…

The pear is a bruise. It looks soft and blue. She wants and doesn't want to touch it. The blood gathers under the blue and the body grows tender, swells, slowly. A greasy kitchen surface. She surveys it with her eyes and a bead of sweat forms on her forehead. And there is a knife. An exact, perfect knife.

She knits her brows into a single dark line, then halves it with the knife. She is misunderstood, like punched dough. Most of all, by her husband. His short, fat fingers, loud mouth. She bites her nails greedily, swallows them. Her food is nails. No need to cook anything from anywhere into anything. Change your life, exchange those bad eggs, sprinkle some flour to cover the smell of damage and sickness.

She is hungry. She knits more brows, handmade brows, more than she can count. She is becoming an expert at home-cooking of hatred. Cuts the meat into chunks, watches them sizzle, adds spices, throws the dice into the pan. Six and two. One and six. Do you really know me. Do you know, I married my first man. Take a chance. The marriage, arranged. And a couple of nothing throws.

She feels a throbbing pain on one side of her face. How the blood gathers under the moon, one giant leap and he doesn't know she eats her own nails, her own half moons. I live under his nail, under his thumb, she thinks. If I could escape, if you can help, please do help yourself to the food. He doesn't know anything personal about her face. His face is a large grainy enlargement when he comes near her and the knife stares at her brows. She stares back at forgetting to eat last night. Again, the knife reminds her. Hot water comes out of the tap and makes a sound like the sound of a siren, while she rinses blood-stained glasses, dishes.

I need scales to measure what I'm missing. One gram of love and some things I can't buy.

The knife stares at her and she touches the blue pear on the side of her face. Things are happening in this kitchen and things are going on, and God help me. She punches a very short number into her mobile phone. "My husband is dead."

THE DISAPPEARANCE

They have been telling her for years: that he went missing in the war, and would you please hold the photo up and keep it still for a few more years? Thank you, ma'am. We will know soon. Then we will really know.

There is not much she does when she is alone. Cooks and thinks, mostly. The photo is gathering dust. And if you look closely, he wears a thin mask made of miniscule fragments of earth, a shred of grass, the foot of an insect, a drop of blood. She wants to make him clean again, especially of the blood.

She waits for them to tell her that a single bone of his body has been found. Then she can finally put the photo down and spend the rest of her life polishing her memories.

She would prefer to hover above her life, like a ghost of her former self, but her feet are heavy, stitched to the ground. The sky fell on her the day they came. She had been baking bread in a wood-fired oven until the flour ran out. There was a knock on the door, and she opened it, still wearing her pale green apron and her smile. Yes? The word froze, the loaves of bread turned black. Yes? They had come to tell her he'd gone missing. It was autumn. Yes?

There is a needle inside her head and she's trying to find it. Why does he look so stern in the photo? Is it because he cannot talk? Tell me everything. Let me make you a coffee. When are you coming back? The fence is broken. The birds are everywhere. My time is running out. But when are you coming back? They keep asking me why I carry this framed photo with me everywhere. Let go, they said, just let go.

It's my husband, can't you see? I replied. And one day he will come knocking at the door.

CACTUS

In the kitchen my mother makes babies with flour and eggs. Her hands and part of her left cheek are covered in white. She bakes the babies so that they can never grow. I look at her and think: I hope I won't look like you twenty years from now, on a day which will be the exact opposite of today.

Some days, the whole house is drunk with secrets. The walls move when my father bangs the door on his way in or out. Mostly out. Once, he tripped on the porch and was sick all over my cactus. Since then, he's talked less and less, as if a cactus spine has got stuck on his tongue.

My bedroom walls are the colour of flamingos. I put up posters with chewing gum and I dance under the fluorescent light for nobody in particular, except maybe myself. I am the only person in the world, the only one in the mirror, the one who understands. Look at me, I say to myself. Just look at me.

My mother eats a cookie, then says a couple of words, then another cookie and another word. She gets fat, fatter, fattest. I want to shake her, so all her complexes will hit the ground, and she'll be new again. A new woman, a new you. Look at you, I want to tell her. Just look at you.

The phone rings, days pass, my father is arrested for drunk driving. The whole world looks at me when I walk down the street wearing my pink ballet shoes. The phone rings for days and days, we don't pick it up. I dance and put up posters, my mother bakes cookies and breaks their heads.

Some days, I want to hug my cactus. I want to cry, to run to another day, to pirouette to the opposite end of my life. Some days, I just want to hide. It gets more and more difficult every day, taking a bow.

We come from the land of the couscous eaters. If you are white, we are dark. We look even darker in daylight, when we go out and sunshine hits our face, like a slap from nowhere. The outside walls of our house aren't

23

pretty peach or lovely lilac like some I've seen when I practise steps on the pavements. They're just walls, kind of dull, white-grey, crumbling here and there.

"What are you doing?" an old lady once asks me, without taking her eyes off my shoes.

"Dancing," I said.

"Is that what you do in your country?" she muttered. "Dance on pavements and obstruct pedestrians?"

"This is my country," I said. "I have an address to prove it."

She walked away, without another word. I wanted to follow her to her house and check out the colour of her walls. Black, maybe. Or sickly melon yellow.

On the day my father gets out of jail, my mother will make couscous. Dad will say it is the second happiest day of his life. He won't say what the first was, but I'll know: the first was when my brother was born.

He was really something, my brother. He worked hard. He went to school, he went to college. He was handsome, all the girls loved him. He was clever, my father was proud. He got a good job, he made money, bought a car. And then one day three years ago, while the sun was just rising, a car crashed into him and he died. The driver of the car was drunk. When they told my father, he stopped talking for months, years. Not a word came out of his mouth, not a single sound. It was as if his voice and his lips had been sewn together by invisible thread.

I play music loudly, to kill the silence. The cactus looks at me. Whenever I dream of my brother, we are in the middle of an orange desert. That's where I dance for him, that's where I burn my feet. He always smiles, always applauds. And I always wake up to darkness before I can even take a bow.

THE AUTHOR AND THE GIRL

The author arrives at the train station in Ciechocinek. He hopes to spend a whole month in summer here, writing and writing. His life is full of knots and he must untie them.

In the kitchen of the restaurant, the girl pounds cinnamon in a mortar. The world is incoherent but she makes perfect sense of it. And when she does, everything smiles.

His hands tremble, he is so fascinated by her. He finds out that one morning, one wild morning, twenty years ago, she was born. Pogrebinsky, Mila. I insist: let me taste your lips, pat you, touch you, smell you, love you, because one day, light years from now, your face will have wrinkles, your lovely heart will be tame, said the author. And I will be a tailor's dummy. You are phosphorescence and a crystal chandelier in my dreams, for now. And she smiled, even though she couldn't hear him think. Her skirt looked amused.

The author makes her a character in his book and centuries later, they meet by Czarny Staw.

Could you move your face a little to one side, please? she asks. I think I know you. I served you soup one cold night. She speaks with a slight accent, clink, clink, clink, as delicate as porcelain.

He doesn't know it yet, but this is the last day of his life.

I wrote a book about you, he tells her. But the story needs another page, another hour. The hero in the book is old, and he's getting older. Can you put his younger face back on? There is also a crack in his heart which you must fill with cinnamon and rosewater.

The girl (who is now a woman) understands. She has lived long enough to know. When the moment comes, when he is suddenly not there and not here, she tiptoes around his empty suit. She searches the pockets for words, paragraphs, pages. Finds nothing. Remembers the night she was a village girl pounding cinnamon in a mortar.

REPUBLIC OF LOVE

I fell over, almost, I lost balance, I saw him. He was carrying the globe in his hands and I could see myself in many years' time, walking with him hand in hand, in Buenos Aires, in Rio de Janeiro, in Auckland, in Vienna, or whichever city his fingers happened to be on right now. My heart was beating so fast it was impossible to think.

Suddenly, everything was green and under threat, and as crowded and lush and dangerous and lovely as the Amazon. It was 8:09 on a warm, humid summer evening. Suddenly, everything and nothing came together. It was the latitude of the place and the longitude of time when I met the explorer called Danny.

I decided to name it the Republic of Love.

Many years later. My soul is trapped in an ice cube. The dream is so cold I wake up shivering. There is a hand on my thigh. My thigh is a hand or a piece of flesh. I cut it out of the picture and something bleeds and my blood freezes. That's how cold it is. My breath floats somewhere above my solitary heater after he's walked out, walked on. I'm still alive, I'm still breathing but yes, my soul is trapped in an ice cube.

I pick up the atlas and look for the Equator. Somewhere warm and tropical to sun myself. Does it really matter where? The Republic of Lost Loves, where ex-couples gather to comfort each other. But it doesn't exist on any map, at least not in this atlas. I've known all along that love is an endangered species, and that you should hold your lover tight, as tight as can be, the way chimps hold their babies to their hairy bodies. I will most likely cry right now. And it will be the warmest rain I've ever felt on my face.

So, I am officially one of those people who walk into hypermarkets or banks and queue up and don't smile for hours. I don't laugh at jokes: she doesn't get it, it is obvious she has a problem.

Something irrelevant always came up in my conversations with Danny. And when it did, Danny looked at me. Just looked at me and didn't say anything. But I knew what he was thinking. He was thinking: What's that got to do with anything? Or: Why did you bring that up just now? Or even: Are you trying to annoy me? But he didn't say a word. That's how much Danny loved me. Enough to take me with all my irrelevancies.

I once wrote a story about a girl on an expedition to the South Pole and I told Danny she must be a courageous girl. She was in her thirties and didn't have an iPod.

What's that got to do with anything? Danny didn't ask.

Well, because on the 900 kilometre expedition from the "Messner start" to the South Pole, on the 28th day out of 40, the girl's iPod broke. She had no music to listen to except the music inside her head, lyrics and music all together in her mind and all that white monotony around her and not a single person in sight. And the girl thought white is such a lonely colour and needed somebody to hold her hand, just to hold her frozen little hand, a bird plucked of its feathers. She carried her dictionary, too.

What do you mean, Danny didn't ask.

I mean that she carried her dictionary around with her, like a bible, everywhere she went, and she wanted to see how far she could get in life without looking up another word in English or any other language. Because you can sometimes guess what a word means just by putting it in your mouth and tasting it, and then saying it out loud. *Acquiescence. Delinquent. Saffron.*

It was really hard for her to live without her love by her side. It was really hard, all that fatigue, 900 kilometres, and no iPod. The girl looked a little like Natalie Portman. During her studies at university she wore a pink wig. She got a First Class Honours. The graduation ceremony went well but she ate and drank too much. And her feet hurt because of the high-heeled shoes.

Danny had no idea what I meant. Are you trying to confuse me? he asked.

She had those shoes on when she kissed her boyfriend for the first time. He was so tall, she wanted to reach him. Longitudes and latitudes. And the last time? All couples remember the last kiss, how it leaves an aftertaste in the mouth, of salt water, and sugar.

Oh, Danny, Danny. There are so many things I want to tell you. If only you were here. But you're in another story. A long time ago story. The relevant part is that I still think of you, you're still, somehow, relevant. I carry you around like a dictionary, a broken iPod, a white song. Maybe one day we will meet again on a flight to Kenya and we will pretend we've never met before. And I will say: You remind me of an ex-boyfriend who was an explorer.

I have put my memories of you and me in a box which I want to seal. Your name is one name in the world I do not want to forget, I do not want to lose. I say it again and again to myself, in the mirror. If you were here, you would laugh, you would ask: What are you doing? I would reply: I am saying your name. You would laugh again: What for? And the answer would be: Because it is a tropical bird which I want to keep in this room, in this house, in my life. And my answer would only make sense to myself. Because nobody else knows that I always lose the one I love.

The man regains consciousness, his scalp burning. And all the time his tears are falling. The man is crying without knowing that he's crying. Ten years ago, when he was still young, when he knew what he was looking for, he never shed a tear. Now he is crying the way men cry: without realizing that the tears are falling, without knowing that they are tears at all, where they come from, and why. He has a vague memory of a lost deal, of the moment somebody decided he should have bad luck. The rest of his life will be a fight against that moment.

The man is now homeless. He dreams like an old man of things past and out of reach. He knows about loss. He knows it is hopeless to be impatient. In fact, he thinks that impatience was a long time ago.

The young woman in the street looks at him with a question on her face: When it rains will you get wet through? He kills time: doing what?

I want to live in a museum, says the homeless person to himself, because I want to be safe. The rain gives him cataract vision, he can't make out any of the words written on the cardboard box he is in.

In another life: the man, clean-shaven and wearing a suit and tie, assuredly walks into a department store, heads for the escalator. He needs to get to the fourth floor, the electronics department, to buy a new charger for his mobile phone. Then, three minutes later, it is exactly 9:09. He has pins and needles in his arms. There is a sudden noiselessness, the people around him turn into smudges. He is drowning. Somebody had turned the hourglass over, somebody is waiting to give him the kiss of life. He has never stood so close to his own soul.

The fountain of life. Rivers converging. Life's strange ways. The three minutes which took everything away from him, except his life. The shape of loss.

The woman walks past the homeless man, walks past him on her way to her house with the pale blue walls. She has a list in her head of things she must do and must not do, of things she must eat and not eat, what she must remember and not remember. She has a bunch of chrysanthemums in one hand and a shopping bag in the other, and balances her body as she steps over a puddle of rainwater. The homeless man looks at her and recognizes something in her.

He wants to show her a scar and make her touch it. The purple blue scar is his line of memory, it is fading. It's the line of extraction, of violent wrenching. I am a piece of floating wood he thinks, I am floating like the cork of a bottle of wine thrown into the river and this line is my journey.

The homeless man is a man with a beard full of knots from the past. He used to be clean-shaven, used to have a wife, a son, a home. He walks, eats nothing, nothing and remembers the members of his family, he was once a man, had a wife, a child. He once had a home. He lives alone by the river. Life is one long river, a pretty voice sings, begins and ends. Ends and begins.

The woman walks away, will soon leave him alone with all that quiet in the night, the stars and the voices in his head. Did you know, he wants to tell her – did you know that seagulls never move their wings? Did you know they fly without flapping their wings? They glide in the air. That there are keys and coins in the river and some people throw in their lives. His hands shake on nights like this when memories jingle like keys on a key-ring. Like ice cubes hitting each other in a glass because there is no space.

He dreams of meeting a woman who will stop, one day. She will have a key in her hand and he will ask her: Is that the key to your house? Can you describe it to me? That's all I want, for you to stop a minute and describe your house to me. She will stare at him and walk on, or she will laugh at him, or she will be disgusted by his long beard and dirty nails. She will turn the other way, walk away. There is nothing I have to tell you, I'm sorry. I'm going home.

Don't be sorry. Is there anybody waiting for you there?

Of course there is. My husband. An explorer. He has packed two suitcases and he's waiting for me to get home. We're setting out on a world tour tomorrow morning. Excuse me, I have to go.

And she turns away, wants to walk away, as far away from him as possible.

Please don't cry, says the homeless man, to her back. Would you like to play cards? I know you're crying, even if I can't see your face. It's the way people turn away when they're crying. And he considers her blue coat, her black boots, her shoulder length dark hair, and the way she's balancing the chrysanthemums and the bag full of shopping in each of her hands.

Teach me something I don't know, he calls to her.

Her heart stops, she turns round and looks at him as if she has just missed a bomb explosion behind her by one second. As if the one extra step she took has decided that she will remain alive, that she has been saved.

What did you say?

I said teach me, says the man.

Teach you what?

Teach me something I don't know.

I don't know what you're talking about.

I don't know what I'm talking about, but I used to write 500-word essays. They were good. Discursive, sometimes descriptive, too. But I'm getting old, I'm cold, I can't remember much about what I learned, I don't know. Can you describe your house to me?

In the beginning. It is the fifth of July, exactly six days before I once met Danny. I live in a house with pale blue walls, the colour of sky. The house has many windows, each of which is a different gilt-framed painting, through which I can see beauty, if I look hard enough.

31

I am reading a letter:

Tomorrow will be the beginning of your life. Tomorrow you will cross a bridge and embark on an authentic journey. Soon, a man will take you 2356 kilometres away from your old life, in a boat smelling of oil and fish and salt. You will wonder when you will ever step out onto the quay of another port, how long it will take before you can put down the two bags containing all your possessions in the world. You're finding it difficult to balance the two, to do a balancing act with the two bags: Keep nothing in your left pocket, empty the right-hand side of your brain of negative thoughts, stop the boat from overturning.

At night, you will both fall asleep together in a small cabin where the wind will blow into your dreams making a hollow sound, a door opening, closing, opening, closing. You will wake up in broad daylight, floating on the ocean, watching a landscape full of lines and wild colours and strange brushstrokes. The earth is full of love and truth, yes, but you know that already, don't you? You will travel in the right direction. It will feel secure, it will feel natural, like the journey of water.

I live in a house with pale blue walls and white furniture. It makes me think I live somewhere near the sky, or that I live in a dream. One could never be angry in this house, but you might feel lonely as you walk from room to room expecting to find something which is never where you last left it. It is not a house designed for one person, not even for two. It is large enough to have an entire family of five or six living happily, filling it with love and laughter.

I inherited the house from an uncle of mine who never married and never had children. He was a dentist. Strange, isn't it, that he made his money from bad teeth, and the only recollection I have of him is this image: him dropping an egg on our kitchen floor, while attempting to make me an omelette.

What's that got to do with anything, Danny didn't ask, when I told him the story.

The egg broke on the floor, made a yellow mess. It somehow never went away, that yellow spot on our kitchen floor –no matter how hard my mother scrubbed. My uncle had left his mark in our house with a broken egg. I was delighted when a tiny eggshell crunched under my feet days later. It was as if a tiny bird had hatched and was sending me a message that I had to decipher. It was a colourful bird which watched me when I wasn't looking, flew in and out of our wide open windows. It travelled and always returned. And once it left me a feather next to my pillow, and I tried to read the feather, I put it in my palm and measured it. It was almost as long as my life line, and I knew there and then that I would love that bird until the day I died.

When I inherited my uncle's house, I spent days inspecting the floor of each and every room, but they were spotless, white, clean. I had lost my bird.

I read the letter again and again. Between its lines is another story.

Tomorrow you will set off on a beautiful journey, a journey you have waited for all your life, the journey you were born for. You must be brave, for you must set off on this journey on your own, with a rucksack containing no dictionary, no map, no compass, just a feather and a letter folded into two.

Danny,

It's been so many years, it's impossible to remember all the details, but I will try. It's hard to be faithful to the original version, to tell it like it was when you set out on a journey into the past.

With my two bags and all my possessions, I am a twenty something in love with a twenty something guy I've just met at university and we want to do what all young couples want to do: travel the world. First explore each other, and then the world, then get married and have children, preferably two, a girl and a boy, and live happily ever after.

How are you, and what are you doing these days? I have often wanted to call you in the middle of the night, just to ask: What happened to your black and white photo of a colony of ants you said you'd like to make into a postcard? I have an old number of yours in an old notebook. I tried calling once but the tone was dead and I knew that number no longer existed. I've stopped trying to locate you ever since. I often wonder if you found your way home, the way I did. Because sometimes birds lose their way too, Danny.

33

I got off the bus last night, and I walked past a homeless man I have seen before. I have never really taken any notice of him except that he has a shockingly thin face and a very long beard, as if all the energy in his face has been sucked up by the beard, every single ounce of his miserable life has gone into that mass of hair. I felt guilty, he looked so cold and desperate. I wanted to say something but I couldn't, I wanted to give him something to eat or drink, I just didn't know how to offer. I kept quiet, pretended I hadn't noticed him.

I just walked on until he said something strange. He said: Teach me something I don't know. And there was something so oddly familiar in his voice, something so unexpected which touched my heart, that I turned sharply round to take a better look at him.

And suddenly, in the dark, like somebody who has reached the end of a tunnel, I went back ten years in time and stared at the gaunt, ghostly silhouette of a man I once used to teach. He was part of a group I taught when I first graduated, on an English course specially designed for businessmen.

So bizarre to think, staring at him in the dark, that he was once one of my best student. That he wrote essays about his family, about the advantages and disadvantages of adopting the euro. He analysed, in good, grammatical English, whole articles in the Financial Times. My heart went white, as if the blood had been sucked out of my body. I felt a sharp pain somewhere next to my right eye. I said "I'm sorry" over and over, until the words wouldn't come out any more. Until I didn't know what else to say, until I couldn't remember how all this had started, and I looked at him and saw his other face. The face from his other life. And I wanted to ask him "But how?" "But why?" but no voice would come out of my mouth, as if I knew no more words. He looked at me, and I knew he knew.

Are you going to teach me? he asked.

I nodded and sobbed in the dark.

I always knew you would come, he said.

I nodded.

I never gave up hope, he said, without looking at me.

I took two steps closer to him, let the flowers and the bag fall somewhere near the puddle. I heard my heart talking to me in a strange language. For once, I didn't reach for the dictionary, I just felt the words and listened to my heart beat, and I knew. For once in my life, Danny, I knew I was doing the right thing. I put my hand on his shoulder and felt him shivering. I moved closer and got down onto my knees and touched his face with my fingertips. With some effort, he raised his own hand to mine and squeezed it with all the energy he could muster. I could hear his breathing and I felt comforted, I felt free.

Finally, Danny, I can tell you what I've been meaning to tell you all these years, to admit what I've never wanted to admit before: I know you are dead. I know I was with you when you died. It was a long time ago, one summer.

The dream is always the same, so cold that I wake up shivering. We are together as a couple, we are together as a team, we have discovered the Republic of Love, the world is envious. The world starts telling me things about you, the world is jealous. I start to look for signs. Impossible, impossible, they are telling me lies, you wouldn't touch that stuff, we will travel the world. The dream is always the same and I wake up shivering. We are together and you tell me you're a bit short of cash and could I lend you some, you're going to buy some books, you're going to study and we're going to travel the world. The dream is always the same and I wake up, every single part of me shaking, the way you were when I last saw you, and I started to scream and I started to scream and I knew you couldn't hear me, you would never be able to hear me, that it was summer and the windows were wide open and the whole world was outside, why, Danny, why, Danny, why, Danny, why did you do this, why did you do this and why are you wearing your yellow T-shirt and what has that got to do with anything, what has anything got to do with anything now that it's all over, you're gone, you're gone...

Are you going to teach me? the homeless man asked.

I nodded and sobbed in the dark.

I always knew you would come, he said.

I nodded.

I never gave up hope, he said, without looking at me.

I live in a house with pale blue walls and white furniture. It makes me think I live somewhere near the sky, or that I live in a dream. One could never be angry in this house, but you might feel lonely as you walk from room to room expecting to find someone who is not there, something which is not where you last left it. It is not a house designed for one person, not even for two. It is large enough for five or six or seven people. It is large enough to offer comfort.

And I said to the bird: Fly in through the window, wash your tired little wings under a dripping tap. I always knew you would come.

TRUTH

At the exact moment my neighbour tells her lover "I'm leaving you," a rainbow appears somewhere behind her. And there's the *ch ch ch* sound in my ear, because I've heard it all before, the truth about how beautiful love was, has been, and so on, and so forth, in the past tense.

Their arguments are always audible, because she raises her voice and he mutes his, and there is a deafening sound in both my ears when she says things like "I've had enough" or "I don't recognise you anymore." Or "Go to hell." Their kitchen window is always open, even in winter.

Right at the beginning, when I first moved in, I thought they might be actors rehearsing a play together at the kitchen table, her voice so clear and deliberate and his pauses so well timed. I listened and listened for clues, but there was always silence after she banged the door. *Any minute now, a champagne bottle will pop, a plate will get smashed, a mirror will break, a tantrum will be thrown, a baby will cry, a canary will sing, any minute now.* But nothing ever happened, and I fell asleep, my ear glued to the pillow. *Ch ch ch, ts ts ts.*

Once, in a dream, her boyfriend hugged me so tight on the stairs, I could hardly breathe. I was on my way down to work, and running late, as usual. It was raining outside and he stopped me on the stairs, held me tight and asked desperately: "Do you hear our arguments? Do you know that I hate her?" I looked at my watch and I looked at his dark, shoulder-length hair and tried to speak but no sound came out of my mouth. "I have nowhere to go," he said, "except hell." And I kissed him on the mouth, and woke up, soaked in rain, flooded in sunlight.

There's my wall, there's their window, there's them. And there's that bitch, Truth, who sniggers at me and makes that sound, *ts ts ts, ch ch ch.* Because, she says, you know what this means, right? You know all about love, don't you? Go and knock on their door, go and tell them.

And here I am, the omniscient narrator. I know everything because I've been through it before. I could tell you so much about my own life but prefer to concentrate on the life of others. It is more civilised, less painful that way.

The truth is, she never loved you. The truth is, you trapped him. It was an illusion, the rainbow was a liar, all those colours were fake. Love is a bubble of emptiness. And one day, years later, you will come face to face with each other on a busy street and there will be no questions asked, because there are no answers.

She tells him "I'm leaving you" and half a pizza grows cold. He counts the olives on its surface waiting for the rest of his life to come.

THE PAST HAS THE FACE OF SIGMUND FREUD

The past never forgets you, remember that.

He sits alone at a small table in the Indian restaurant, and eats and thinks. He looks exactly like Sigmund Freud. It could be him. The same forehead, the same nose, the same beard, the same glasses. It must be him. The same harsh voice.

"Who are you?"

"Don't you know me?"

"Who are you?"

"Don't you recognise me?"

"I like your hair. Curly. But I don't recognise you at all."

"Could we have met in a dream?"

"Ah, perhaps."

"You said you would never forget me."

"Tell me about it. Slowly. I am still on my starter."

It is a vegetable samosa. One tiny little samosa. He has not even bitten into it yet.

And I start telling him about my dream. The dream from long ago, how we bumped into each other on Berggasse in Vienna, how he shook me in the middle of the street as if I had pockets full of coins that he wanted. How he ranted and raved because I had made him late for an appointment.

"Do you remember?"

"No. No. But go on."

So I do go on. There was a crowd of people around us. He was still shaking me, swearing, but not letting go. "Let go of me!" I screamed. "Just let go of me, you madman!" and people just watched helplessly, stood around us like statues in a park, a beautiful, lush green Viennese park on the banks of the Danube. "You whore!" he cried. "You look just like…" And then he stopped, as if he'd just woken up, dropped his arms to his sides, picked up his briefcase, and walked away.

I've always wanted to know the ending of the story. The last word.

"Who do I look like?"

"Who?"

"Who do I remind you of?"

"Remind? Nobody that I can think of."

The waitress picks up the small plate where the vegetable samosa had been. The plate is a deep burgundy colour, and empty.

"I was pregnant when you shook me."

"Shook you? Where?" For the first time, he looks up from the menu.

"In the middle of Berggasse."

The name of the street. That street. The past never forgets.

"You shook me hard, hard, harder, harder. And later that night –"

"Yes?"

" – I lost the baby."

Both sides of the menu are also a deep burgundy embellished with gold letters and pseudo-Indian motifs. His face is stone cold. But his heart is blushing, I know it. It is pumping hard, I feel it. Hard, harder, harder.

"Who are you?"

"How dare you?"

"How dare you disturb my meal with this – with this – preposterous dream?"

"It wasn't just my dream. You were in it."

"Did you wake up?"

"Yes."

"Did your life change?"

"Yes."

"For the better?"

"Yes."

"How?"

"I forgot about you."

"Then please leave me alone. Please leave me alone. You are a beautiful woman, but I want to eat this curry on my own."

There is something about this stranger's face which attracts me to him, but his attitude repels me. I am somebody he knows and despises, someone he doesn't know and loves. I was his sister-in-law, he is my former lover. I miscarried his child.

We have never met before. Or, if we have, it was a long time ago.

"You look just like her." His voice sounds different, more gentle, more human.

I turn round.

"Who?" I am waiting for the last word. "I look like who?"

"The woman of my dreams."

THE BOOK OF DESPERATE DREAMS

I started recording dreams when I realised that my dreams were so colourful, so vivid and so desperate I could write a whole book about them. I wrote them in my notebook every morning when I woke up, and read them out to my therapist every afternoon. He looked at me long and hard and asked me questions about them. Mostly dull, uninteresting questions, as if he'd never had a dream in his life.

"So you want me to come true?" asks the dream. "Yes, I whisper. "Uh-huh. Uh-huh," to the pillow. Even in my sleep, I can't find the right words, except yes, yes, uh-huh, uh-huh, but I cling to the idea that the dream may, one day or night, in summer, spring, autumn or cold winter, come true.

"Do you talk in your sleep?"

"Yes, but I was talking to a dream. And last night, a bird spoke like a human. Or a human spoke like a bird. I can't remember. It was a colourful parrot –bird of paradise –parakeet kind of dream. Papageno. A soprano, a mezzo-soprano and a contralto voice kept asking what I wanted most in life. Papapapapapageno? they shrieked. Papapapageno, I replied."

"But what does it mean?"

"The dream?"

"No, the word."

"Which word?"

"Papageno."

"I think it means parrot, but I'm not sure."

"So, what is it you want most in life?"

"Papageno, which means a parrot. Which could also mean: twist my fate. Which could also mean: fuck-all. Which could also mean: love."

A few days later I told him about a wonderful dream where I was having sex with the man I've always wanted to have sex with. I wanted this so badly, thought about it day and night, and finally it happened. In a dream. Yes, yes and yes. Uh-huh. But. I woke up and everything was lost. The man, his body, everything.

"Can you describe the man?"
"No."
"Why not?"
"I can't. I shouldn't."
"Who is he?"

"He's a friend of my father's. I like the smell of his aftershave and the way he looks at me."

I was in New York and I was Suzanne Vega. My hair was long and straight, my lips were luscious and ruby-red with lipstick and I sang a song nobody had ever heard before. It was about love, the kind of love you only read and dream about and never, ever actually experience. I went to bed with love in my arms and I slept uninterrupted till morning. It was strange but beautiful. I woke up and I started writing and words flowed. The pages ended, I had so much to write about.

"I had so much to say. Then I woke up."

"Do you remember the song?"

"No, but my lips looked just like Suzanne Vega's. And I was smiling."

My dreams are diaries of my days, of my life. Some are vastly empty, unbelievably boring. Others have haunting voices, cruel scenarios which expect me to do things like dance while ash is getting into my eyes. I put all the memories together with elastic bands, stretching as far as the elastic will go. Sometimes the elastic band breaks and I abandon my decisions and panic, like a rabbit which is about to be massacred, like a terrible secret which is about to be discovered and cut into like cake, cake, not bread, but cake.

"I was looking for a bakery which sells bread during Pesach. It is an impossible dream. Let them eat cake, cake, not bread but cake."

And once I said: "I would like you to be a part of my dreams, one day or night. Please hurry."

43

"Who are you talking to?"

"I'm talking to myself."

"Is everything all right?"

"Of course. Why shouldn't it be?"

"Why are you talking to yourself in the second person singular?"

"Why shouldn't I?"

"There are rules, grammar rules, you know."

"Yes, I know, but there are no rules in dreams, you know. It was summer and the sky was sky blue. What a lovely sky and so polite!"

"How can the sky be polite?"

"The sky can be anything you want it to be. If you're happy and you know it clap your hands. And suddenly, a thunderclap, and everything changes, as things do, in a dream. Rain, raindrops, as big as rose petals and the floor slippery and then tears filling the bucket, falling off the face of that lovely, polite sky. The sky can be anything you want it to, even a face."

The face of a lover from years ago often appears to me in dreams. He tells me I am his Song of Songs, his Dream of Dreams. I still love you, he says.

My mother was making jam. It was too red to be true. Like pulped strawberries, raspberries and red paint and hearts and period blood all together as one. This is love, she was saying. But I knew better. It was turning yourself inside out. It was beauty. It was a moment. It was a gift. It was your body. For him. To drink.

"Do you often dream of having sex?" he asked calmly. Too calmly.

"Are you jealous?"

I woke up at 9:56 am the next day and tried to reconstruct the dream. No matter how hard I tried, the dream had gone. Sometimes I chase dreams, the meaningful ones, for the meaning of life. This morning there was no meaning, it evaporated when I opened my eyes. There was a heavy blanket on top of me and I was clasping my pillow. The only meaning I could find was that night is infinitely connected to morning and that morning is infinitely connected to night.

Some of my dreams are exhibitions of lines. Like the map of a library of 300,000 books where you're looking for one book whose title you've forgotten. There is a slow-moving queue of people who have lined up to find that same book. Follow, follow, follow each other, like sheep, sheep, sheep. The world is exactly as it is outside the dream and we all know, really, that there is no such book. There is no book called "The Book of Desperate Dreams".

"Why did you call it that?"

"Because my dreams are desperate. And there is nothing I can do to stop them. And there is nothing I can do about it."

"Are you seeing a therapist?"

"Yes, and he looks at me calmly. Too calmly."

SPARROW

My sister said she was carrying a bird inside her, a bird which would soon be drinking water out of her navel. I wasn't supposed to say anything about it. To anyone.

"I am a cage," said my sister. "Inside me I keep secrets, inside me I keep a bird." And she laughed and I laughed, too. We laughed until we no longer remembered what we were laughing about.

"His name is Sparrow," she said one day. "He's only little now, as tiny as a seed – but he'll grow and grow, you'll see. And then I'll set him free." She placed her hand on her stomach and her mouth curved upwards, as if she were smiling at another world in the mirror.

I couldn't wait. Time was too still, it was taking too long. I squinted into the future. "When?" I kept asking. "When, when, when?" My sister looked luminous as she replied: "Soon, soon, soon." She said he was practising a song for us. "He'll sing it so well that he will astonish us all."

Time passed. I rode my bike and I skipped and whistled and played and waited. Sparrow was going to be my small gift for keeping my sister's secret. The air grew heady and my sister soft and heavy, like ripening fruit. When she fluttered her eyelids, I thought she was dreaming with her eyes open.

It was the longest summer. My sister turned sixteen. She wore a long, flowery dress, put her hair up in a ponytail. There were sixteen pink and red balloons bobbing around her head that hot, sticky afternoon of cake, cellophane and candles. My mother spoke loudly and happily about nothing and everything, my stepfather handed my sister the knife, helped her cut the cake. Then she said: I have an announcement to make.

And the world stops there, a sharp intake of breath.

I squint into the past now for details, terrified of what I might remember. The sky is a dazzling blue, the earth hot, sweaty. I am pregnant, says my sister. She wears a necklace of grapes with which she will feed

Sparrow. She performs her own birthday song beautifully, she sings her heart out – until her throat is chalk dry and her ribcage breaks. There are feathers everywhere. I run to pick them up as the balloons pop one after the other, leaving sixteen pieces of rubbery flesh on the floor, things torn and shapeless, parts of my sister which will never again be whole.

I sit beside her and ask if it hurts. She whispers: "Truth always hurts." Then there is a sudden, white silence which reminds me, years later, that she is no longer here.

LEMONS, STARS

We woke up and played games in the middle of the night.

"Let's go outside," my sister said. "I want to be in the garden."

I followed her shadow into the kitchen, out the door. When we reached the lemon tree she said: "When I grow up, I want to be a star." I laughed.

There were too many lemons on that tree. I said: "Let's pick some lemons."

She giggled. "You don't come out into the garden at night to pick lemons," she said. "You come out to pick stars." Then we giggled together. Silently. Trying not to wake the world.

There really were too many lemons. They looked cold and unreal in the moonlight. My sister said: "I want to play." So we played this game of make-believe: that she was a star which had landed in the lemon garden to tell me a secret from another world. That I was a lemon which could talk, and there were others like me. That one of the lemons on the tree was evil – and we didn't know which one.

My sister said we should climb the tree. I said it was impossible, she would fall. She climbed it anyway. When she said she'd touched the evil lemon, I pulled her down as fast as I could. "You touched the bad lemon!" I hissed. "You touched it!"

She giggled and started running back towards the house. I looked at my hand, at her and the stars. We went to bed as if nothing had happened.

When they discovered the tumour in her brain a few months later, I imagined it had the same shape as the lemon she had touched: rotting, going bad. It kept me awake for nights on end. Once, when the whole house was asleep, I walked out into the garden, kicked the tree and spat at the stars.

48

UNBORN

The first time I meet him, he asks for a glass of water, but it is my own throat which feels dry and constricted. His face is a moon, white. In a crystal clear voice he asks if I can hear him, says that I shouldn't ignore him, that he needs water. I walk as fast as I can without looking back. I walk out of the dream, and wake up.

In the second dream, it is his hair which is shocking in its whiteness. The background is green, the colour of rain-washed, clean grass. You didn't let me grow, he says, and points an accusing finger at me. He then turns round and walks away. My heart pounds with the word Guilt a hundred times in the dark.

The third and last. We are in a room which smells of the pulp of some over-ripened, fallen fruit. This is where I live, he says. Forever. As he approaches me, I can see that he is not my child, but the neighbours' little boy, the one who limped. Look at me, he cries, and waves a piece of thread in front of his face. You cut me out because I was wrong.

There are times when I search for the end of the thread, all of a sudden cold and empty and shivering inside. I am the mother of the lost boy. I am not a mother. There is no boy. He is lost. He is not a boy. He is Unborn. And all my days go backwards, blending each other into complete whiteness, a blank.

THE JOURNEY

The worst part of the journey was over, Katerina thought, pushing the key into the hotel room lock. It had not been an easy flight, for a number of reasons. There had been an unexpected delay, she'd been charged extra because the dimensions of her suitcase were not right, and, worst of all, she'd had to sit through the whole flight listening to the woman next to her. She had marital problems, her husband was always working late, her son was being bullied in the army. Katerina thought, more than once during the woman's monologue, that she looked like a Chihuahua: big eyes on a tiny face, a latent aggression in her voice, a kind of futile ferocity in the way she moved her hands when she spoke.

She had a splitting headache, her eyes were sore. "Lack of sleep is enough to make you crazy." She remembered reading that, somewhere, a long time ago. It had been suggested that they'd be going to a local restaurant on the evening of their arrival but she could think of nothing worse. She was tired, needed a shower and a rest. She wondered if they'd all think she was antisocial if she actually said that out loud: "I'm tired. I need a shower and a rest." Would they look at her with surprise, dismay, even scorn? The conference was, after all, a short break for all of them, and her colleagues from the Archaeology department all felt they'd worked hard for it. Who would want to miss out on a visit to Athens for a few days? She considered a different wording: "I'm sorry, my stomach's playing up again/Sorry guys, I'm having an early night/Tomorrow?" but said none of those things, because none of them had actually asked if she was going to join them. Not yet, anyway.

She placed the suitcase on the rack and unlocked it. Then she glanced at herself in the long, rectangular mirror. She looked as tired as she felt. Perhaps she shouldn't have come after all, in her condition. She hadn't told anyone yet, felt there was no need to. Taking off her coat and scarf, she examined her body, noted that her legs looked much thinner than they had ever done before, that her upper body had filled out earlier than she had expected. Five weeks, the doctor had said. She wondered what she'd forgotten to pack this time. "The dress," she muttered to herself. "I forgot the dress on the ironing board." Her phone rang just as she was finishing unpacking. She did not immediately recognise the number. A vaguely familiar voice at the other end said: "Katerina, it's me, George. Please call me back. I have news about your father."

She did not call back. She didn't want to. She spent the whole evening thinking about the futility of it all. They had waited for years to know what had happened to her father, her mother refusing adamantly to accept that he was long dead. 'News', George had said. It almost made her cry. She imagined that her father's bones had been discovered in a mass grave. That while a foetus was gestating in her own womb, her father's bones were being extracted from the dry, chalky earth as if in an archaeological dig. Her mother had been six weeks pregnant when her father had disappeared, had gone missing in the war which divided the island and its soul. All through the night the image of her father's bones kept her awake. White bones in the moonlight, ghosts from the past before her past.

She felt ill during her presentation the next day.

"You look pale," Michael had said at breakfast. "Are you all right?"

"Yes, thanks, just tired," she'd replied.

Now, a few hours later, during this important talk she had to give in front of hundreds of delegates from around Europe, her legs suddenly felt weak, a slight nausea travelled up to her mouth, and her voice became tremulous. "I'm sorry," she managed to say, breaking into a sweat. "I'm not feeling very well."

She stepped down from the podium, and a couple of the organisers rushed towards her, one placing his hand on the small of her back, another leading her to the closest chair. Involuntarily, she looked at Michael, who was sitting on the front row. He was worried, she knew that, because his eyebrows were knit together and his right foot was twitching, in the way it often did when he felt uneasy. If he'd stood up and gone to her then, the secret game they'd been playing for months would be over.

In an ideal world, it would have been a dream come true: Katerina pregnant with the man she loved. In real life, things were different, all terribly wrong. She had already decided she would tell him, but not the whole story. She'd have liked to announce it to the whole department, as part of her paper. *Michael and I… Dr Patterson and I… You see, we… It couldn't be helped…* A casual twist of the knife, while watching the twitch of his right foot get more and more impatient. *And, by the way, I'm pregnant.*

They called a taxi but, on the spur of the moment, instead of giving the address of the hotel, she asked to be driven to the Acropolis. For a while, she just stood at the bottom of the sacred rock and, looking up at the unique perfection of the monument, she inhaled the afternoon. A recollection came to her out of nowhere: of her standing in the garden of her childhood home, looking up at the sun until it blinded her. The temporary blindness had made her feel she'd entered another world, a world where her father existed but could not be seen. She thought about perfection in an imperfect world. She could feel the tears forming at the corners of her eyes and struggled with them for a few seconds before they fell. Standing on the same spot for what seemed like hours, she knew that despite the noise and the commotion and uncertainty around, somewhere inside her was a being which was calm, and perfect, and beautiful. And only then did she realise she was not alone.

THE GENTLEMAN ON THE TRAIN

Did any of this happen? I ask myself. I live in a haze these days. Haze, daze, I don't know, same thing. Somebody smiles at you and you think everything's oops-a-daisy. And that somebody is a gentleman: blue-blooded, clean-shaven, well-off, gentle yet strong, every woman's dream.

Let me start at the beginning, or what I think is the beginning. The gentleman discreetly eyes my cleavage at intervals as we travel together from London to Manchester. We are not travelling together, as a couple. We just happen to be on the same train. He happens to be sitting opposite me. I happen to be a size 34C. He looks up from his Financial Times and smiles at me from time to time. I think he is a gentleman.

"Going to Manchester?" he asks.

"Yeah."

"Live there?"

"No, visiting my boyfriend."

"Ah… Tell me about him. Been with him long?"

This shouldn't be happening, but it is. What does he care? And why should I tell him? Should I just tell him to mind his own business? Or…

"We've been together for… er, about a year now…"

"About a year…That's nice. And what's he done to deserve a smashing girl like you?"

Smashing girl. I'm a smashing girl, and I don't even know it, because nobody's ever called me a smashing girl before. I can just see myself going round smashing men's hearts and denting their lives with a hammer and asking them what they've done to deserve me.

"What's he done to deserve me?" I laugh. "I don't know. He loves me, that's all. He …says he loves me."

"…That's all?"

"Well, what else is there?"

"There should be more to a relationship than your boyfriend just saying he loves you…"

While my fellow passenger is saying this, my mind's doing a fast rewind of the past year and I'm thinking: Shit, when did he tell me that he loves me? I made that up. We're just…We just sleep together, that's all. We sleep together and we live apart, and I don't even know what he gets up to on weekdays when I'm not with him and he's supposed to be studying and I'm supposed to be working, and everything's supposed to be Okay.

"Do you love him?"

"What do you think?"

"I think you're incredibly sexy."

"Are you flirting with me?"

"What do you think?"

So I dump my boyfriend there and then, so to speak, in an almost empty compartment on a train and smile an oops-a-daisy smile at the gentleman. I may even be blushing at the same time.

But let me start at the beginning. The gentleman is discreet, but his eyes wander from his paper at intervals as we travel together from London to Manchester. We happen to be on the same train and he happens to be sitting opposite me. I happen to be a size 34C. He looks up from his Financial Times and smiles shyly at me from time to time. And then I decide to open my big mouth.

"Where you from?"

"Pardon?"

"Where are you from?"

Hesitation hangs in the air. "Originally? From Windsor," he says. And adds even more hesitantly, as if he's tiptoeing into some unknown territory: "I – live in Surrey."

"Oh, right. So you're on a business trip to Manchester?"

"Er, not really."

"Travelling for pleasure, then?"

There's a tiny, ever such a slight, loss of self-control in his eyes. And he lets out a small, embarrassed cough, which he hopes will cover his next two words. "Not exactly."

"What 'exactly', then?" I ask, looking him straight in the eye. "Why can't we Brits say exactly what we mean? Why do we always have to beat about the fucking bush?"

It's come out all wrong and I have an urge to laugh. The thought of a bush for that purpose!... I can almost read his mind. Should he pretend he hasn't heard and carry on beating about the... reading about the ... latest crisis in the Financial Times? In the end, he lets out a chortle.

"I'm sorry, your name...?"

"Sharon. Yours?"

"John."

"Are you married, John?"

"Yes." Monosyllabic, gentlemanly.

"Just yes? Is that it?"

"Well... What else is there to say?"

"Describe your wife to me, for example. Where did you meet? How long have you been together? How many kids? What kind of car does she drive?"

"A Volvo."

"I see."

"What?"

"What do you mean?"

"What do you see, exactly?"

"Exactly? Okay, I'll tell you exactly what I see, because I can read minds, you know. In your mind I see a beautifully detached house where everybody lives a detached kind of life. Two kids, a son and a daughter who go to school. A detached wife who doesn't really remember when or why she was ever attached to her husband who doesn't really want to know anything about anything other than what's written in the paper, can't detach himself from the Financial Times... I'm sorry... I – I'm just being rude. I'll just shut up for the rest of the journey."

"No, don't."

"Sorry..."

"You weren't being rude, honest. You're honest... I mean, you're right. And you're also..."

"Yeah?"

"I think..."

55

"What?"

"You're very sexy."

So he divorces his wife there and then, so to speak, in an almost empty compartment on a train. He smiles at me, and he blushes. It's rather sweet of him to blush.

So let me start at the beginning. The gentleman eyes my breasts from time to time as we travel together from London to Manchester. We aren't travelling together, we just happen to be on the same train and he happens to be sitting opposite me. I happen to be a size 34C. At times, he looks up from his Financial Times and smiles at me. He seems like a gentleman. Neither of us speaks throughout the journey. It's a game I like to play, and the gentleman plays it to perfection.

SMIRNOFF SAYS

Alexei said later it was the vodka that did it. It went to his head and made him say and do things he wouldn't normally do or say.

Alexei had another vodka. "Please," he said.

"Please what?" asked the barmaid.

"Just please. Please, please, whatever, please. In England people say please and thank you and thank you and please. So maybe I said please instead of thank you. Sorry."

He looked admiringly at his glass of pure, neat pleasure. The liquid cleared his throat and burnt a hole in his soul and reminded him of so many things he was trying to forget.

The barmaid went on polishing wine glasses and ignoring him. The art of ignoring, she'd perfected that some time ago. If Alexei had a heart attack, she would probably ignore him, because heart attacks were none of her business and she knew nothing about them. She knew more about heat stroke and, strangely enough, she was thinking about beach holidays in Lanzarote when she realised that Alexei had left his seat and was now hiding under one of the tables, crying. "Please," he was saying, "please, let me hide here, don't find me. Thank you, don't find me. I hate her." It was the harshest, most Russian H he could bring himself to utter: "I hate her."

The ice cube lady, the one he hated and was married to, the one whose cheeks sank in as if she were sucking ice cubes all the time, always said she did everything out of love for Alexei. When she spoke about him, she shortened him to Alex. He didn't like that. "Alexei!" he repeated, correcting her. "Not Alex – Alexei! I am not British, not American, but Russian!"

The barmaid looked at him, tried to ignore him, but couldn't.

57

In his head, the ice cube lady was saying: "Now, now, Alex. Remember what we said about the H's? It hasn't been that long." She stood in front of him sucking ice cubes and repeating over and over, "Remember? Remember, Alex?"

"Alexei!" he screamed. "Not Alex, Alexei!"

The barmaid was interested and not interested. "Alexei?" she said, more to herself than to him.

"Yes," he replied. "Alexei. Alexei Smirnoff."

"What? As in Smirnoff vodka?"

"No, Alexei Vodka Smirnoff, please."

"Uh-huh."

"You want to know why?"

"Why what?"

"Why my second name Vodka? Because I live with ice cube! Of course!"

And then he started laughing: a demented laughter which made her look up at him, and then look back down at her hands.

"Let me explain," said the ice cube lady, the way she always explained things to her psychologist. "Alex and I met in a pub in London about two years ago. Since then we have become friends, lovers, and married arch-enemies, in that order. He hates me because I'm trying to make him something that he isn't, or so he says. I hate him because he acts like a Russian peasant whenever we're out with friends. The more he speaks, the more I want him to shut his mouth, the more vodkas he drinks, the more I loathe him, the more I cringe, the more I suck in my cheeks and the more he wants to slap me, or so he says. When we first met, we used to play 'Simon Says'. He'd never heard of such a game before in his life and found it hilarious. Simon says: Kiss me, kiss me. No, Simon says: Fuck me, my beautiful tsar, screw me, yes, yes, yes, please. Simon says, I said. And we laughed."

Alexei dragged himself to an armchair near the bar and managed to sit down. "I hate her," he told the barmaid. "We meet, we marry, I don't know nothing. No English, nothing. Just work and say yes and no and sorry. So I learn some English, I make her laugh, she take me home one night to beautiful apartment, everything clean and beautiful and crystal, it was … how you say… fairy-tale. I am Alexei, I am tsar, she princess, English princess…"

The barmaid now turned round to listen to him, as if he were really telling her a fairy-tale. His broken English, his bits and pieces of words and pauses and sobs seemed to make some sense to her. She remembered the time she had stolen money, just so her five-year-old sister could dress as a princess and go to a fancy dress party. It was a mistake she was always running away from. *Please don't find me, please, please. I'm somebody else, I'm not me.*

"Here," she said, handing him the ice cube bucket. "Have one. To make you feel better."

Alexei put an ice cube into his mouth. Then he took a gulp of vodka. He did it again, and again, until he couldn't feel his tongue or the walls of his mouth any more. Another ice cube, more vodka, and the days of his life, backwards.

"I am travelling back to my life," he said to the barmaid.

She tried to smile at him.

"Alexei says, thank you. I am happy, sad, I am laughing, crying. Thank you and please."

She liked the way his face looked distorted through the glass she was drying. "Yeah," she said, and nodded. "I know what you mean. Sometimes, nothing makes any sense. Not a single fucking thing."

She thought of the cold outside the door, of her boots sinking into the lonely snow path that led to the car park. *I'm somebody else, I'm not me,* she thought. And for a moment she wondered what would happen if she and Alexei were the only two people in the world. If he'd follow her to her car and sing her a Russian song. If they'd dance and collapse on the carpet of snow, totally drunk, and totally happy. And if sobriety was, in fact, contrary to popular belief, simply a kind of performance.

ORIGAMI

My mother's hands are always moving, making things, touching, cutting. There are decorations hanging from different ceilings in our house: dangling mobiles, chimes, charms, ornaments. Origami dragons. I'm not sure where I come into all this, into her fantasy world, except that she gave birth to me, that we live together, that she tries and tries to make me happy.

I put on a play once, when I was seven. I called it "The Beauty of the Beast" and invited my friends from school to take part. There were no written words, the actors were to improvise. "The important thing is the title," I said. "Everything else is irrelevant." My mother was delighted. "Beautiful title! Little angel!" she exclaimed as she walked round the living room puffing up a cushion, picking a piece of thread off the carpet, straightening a frame.

The show was a hit. My friend Chloe was the beauty, Isabelle was the owner of a beast. They found each other one day, while walking their dogs. Chloe said "You're a beautiful Doberman, will you let me touch you?" Isabelle smiled: "My dog is a Doberman and if you look closely, you will see the beauty in his eyes." My mother laughed and laughed. "Geniuses!" she cried. "That was the best show ever!" She clapped her hands together and got up to bring cupcakes and lemonade.

When I remember that I have no father my heart leaps into my throat. Somebody sets the living room on fire. That's when the conversations start.

"I love you, Daddy," I say over and over.
"Who're you talking to?"
"The beast."
"Why are you so late, Daddy?"
"Who are you talking to?"
"No one."
"Daddy, you smell of cigarettes."

"What are you doing?"

"Talking to my dad."

My father left us ten years ago, just before I was born. My mother waited all these years to inform me, kissed me on the cheek one day and told me. She added: "We're better off without him. We'll be fine, darling, don't worry." She hugged me, and her skin was soft, her hair smelled of shampoo. When she looked at me afterwards, could she see she'd wrenched something out? She'd probably never know exactly what it was.

"I thought Dad was dead," I said. "That's what you told me."

"I never told you that," she said, looking at me with concern.

"No, but I thought that. You made me think that."

"I'm sorry, darling," she replied. "You weren't old enough to know. But now you are. He left us."

She'd killed my father with three words. HE. LEFT. US. And I would hate her for not having told me the whole story before, for thinking that as long as she hid the ugly truth, for as long as I lived with her within these walls made of paper and glitter, everything was pretty, everything was perfect. Everything was origami.

I close my eyes and I imagine my father. He is a man with an honest face, twinkling eyes and dark skin. He tells jokes and makes people laugh. He smokes cigarettes and makes perfect bacon and egg breakfasts. He is probably a pilot, travels from country to country with his uniform on and smiles as he announces to the passengers: "Ladies and Gentlemen, we are now landing in Tokyo. Look out for the dragon."

Once, in a land of mythical creatures, once in Japan, there lived a dragon. It had the thick, green, scaly body of a reptile, blazing eyes, long claws which dug deep into the earth and bored holes through secrets long buried. It was a good-looking beast which performed on special occasions, it swallowed and spat out fire, putting on a show of mock bravery, of explosions of its inner self, flames which curled and got bigger and bigger, wilder and wilder, threatening to engulf everything around and burn it into ash. "The dragon has angry breath," somebody said. People watched in horror and ran away, pulling their children away by the arms, got into their cars, rushed back to safety.

School holidays are the worst, the longest. When my mother can't handle things, she'll shove them under the carpet, we never talk about important things, never discuss matters that need to be discussed. It's as if she's looking at her life through a keyhole and doesn't know where the key is. She complains about losing a pair of scissors, or a tube of glue, never about losing that key, the most important thing in her life.

I stare into the future and wonder what would happen if I ran away. I'd leave her a note, saying I've gone to find Dad, I'll be back. She'd panic, open and close the fridge, straighten a fridge magnet, start crying, call the police, in that order. "My daughter's missing. My daughter, Anna, she's gone... I've no idea... She didn't say." Meanwhile I'd be eating bacon and eggs with Dad, chewing and talking at the same time. We'd be in a kitchen devoid of any gadgets and trinkets, just a table and three chairs, a fridge, grey cupboards and a grey floor, a built in oven, a stool. My father would be telling me stories about his travels, complaining that he hardly has any time for himself, his schedule is overloaded, would I like to travel with him, where to. I would forgive him everything. It wasn't his fault he left us, he had to do it. After all, he is a pilot and that's what pilots do, fly away.

Once, in a land of mythical creatures, once in Japan, there lived a dragon. People said it had been cursed to set things on fire. The cherry trees were in bloom and the lake in the garden looked picture perfect. You could see the reflection of a golden temple in the water, and the vast greenness gave the landscape such tranquillity you'd think you were in paradise.

The dragon did not want to destroy it all. No, it didn't. But there are things you do which you can't help doing, can't stop from happening. And so when the first branch of a fir tree caught fire, there was no stopping it. It was like the beginning of a terrible pain that overtakes one's organism, a fight which gets out of control, an aeroplane that goes out of orbit. Nobody, nothing can stop it. When the branches turn black and the lake reflects a blazing forest and a blackening sky, the dragon thinks: "I didn't mean it, I'm sorry."

When I told the therapist I wanted to burn our house down, he asked me to name a few of the positive things in my life. "Eggs and bacon," I replied. "The way the oil sizzles in the pan." He went on to ask me if I'd ever want to meet my dad.

"I meet him every day," I replied.

"Really? Where?"

"After school, he picks me up."

"And what do you do together?"

"Depends. Sometimes we go shopping together. Sometimes he helps me with homework. Next summer, he's taking me to Japan with him. Japan or Australia."

Dr Stevenson wrote things down. He knew nothing about me except what I told him, and I knew nothing about him except that he reminded me of an owl.

My mother says there is nothing she can't make out of paper. She folds the colourful paper expertly, and within minutes she has produced crabs, swans, monkeys, cranes, roses, cats. They sit on her desk with their angular bodies and wings, are strewn around the house like creatures from another planet, creatures sent to discover how humans live.

LA DOLCE VITA

There was a museum hush hush in the living room. My mother said "Butterflies break, you know," and then "Do you remember Auschwitz?" and finally, before another long silence: "Don't you etcetera me!"

There was a pain in my throat, like a lodged sweet. When she came out with "La Dolce Vita!" it sounded like a treasure she'd dug up, but I carried on staring at the same page, same line in my book. She finally muttered: "Sew your dreams together and see what happens."

In a dream, my mother and I are hugging each other. I can smell her hair and body odour and stale perfume as I pour out my soul in sobs onto her face, her neck, her shoulders. "I didn't tell you things I meant to. I kept things from you. I'm ashamed I didn't love you until you made no sense."

And my heart is beating erratically, like long, strange, jumpy words out of context. In-cur-able, in-comp-re-hen-sible. I can feel the butterfly breaking, scraps of its dead wings shrivelling in the wind, ideas gone, found, gone. The unimaginable sadness of forgetting, the bitter sweet.

In another dream, my mother tells me a secret about her youth and asks me to live with it. When I look at her, her face is mine. We're sitting in a living room I've never seen before, and she's sewing syllables together: Ausch-witz. Et-ce-te-ra. La Dol-ce Vi-ta. I am not yet born. The story has not begun, but this is its beginning. I know it, I know it in my heart.

THE SUITCASE

I patted the suitcase all the way to Ben-Gurion airport. Almost as if I were carrying a child that needed reassurance: don't worry, everything's gonna be fine. Everything will be *beseder*, beseder? No one's going to touch you baby, you're mine. I think I even drummed it once or twice with my fingers. And refused an offer of help carrying it. It must have looked heavier than it was. Do you need help? the man sitting next to me asked. I probably do, I replied, but not with carrying the suitcase. He probably thought I was mad. Which I probably am.

At the airport, I think it was the eyeliner. I blame it on the eyeliner, too dark, too much kohl. Shouldn't have put so much on. I don't know, it probably made me look suspicious. So they asked me all kinds of questions before I even got to the check-in desk. And even though I was wearing my little lucky 'hamsa' charm, you could say it turned out to be quite an unpleasant day.

First it was the female security officer, trying to sound polite. Staring into my kohl-rimmed eyes, thinking she can make me crumble.

What are you carrying in the suitcase?

In the suitcase? Documents.

Documents? What kind of documents?

What kind of documents? Papers. Letters. Of a personal nature. For my eyes only.

Please open the suitcase.

Open it? I just told you it's private. You're invading my privacy.

Miss, open the suitcase. *Bevakasha.*

So I did. I opened it in the space of four syllables. Be-va-ka-sha. Because it didn't sound like a request at all. More like a command.

Look, I said. Papers, just like I told you. Old letters. Lieber Franz. Lieber Max. Old German letters. Danke. Bitte. Be-va-ka-sha.

Do you speak German?

A little.

And Hebrew?

A little, very little.

I see. Where did you acquire these letters? Did somebody give them to you? Did you pack the suitcase yourself?

No. I mean yes, I packed it myself. I mean no, nobody gave them to me...

And how did they come to be in your possession?

I bought them.

Bought?

Yes, and they cost me a few shekels.

At this point, she signalled to two more officers, one male, one female. One of them (female) closed the suitcase. The other (male) lifted the suitcase and said Follow me. I've always known that those two words (three syllables) spell out trouble:

Fo– llow. Me.

So I had to sit in a room with both of them sitting at a desk facing me, and I had to tell them what happened from the very beginning. How, in the very beginning, a week ago, I told my Israeli boyfriend that on my first visit to Tel Aviv I wanted to go for a walk in old Jaffa. How he advised me to just chill out and go to the beach instead, how I insisted that I've always wanted to go to Jaffa, so we should do it together. How he gave in and finally agreed. I haven't been to Jaffa for years, he said. But I'll do it for you. So we went all the way up the hill, up the stairs, into little alleys, past the shop where they sell the most incredibly intricate 'hamsot', over the wishing bridge, past that charming restaurant called Bernhardt Show, (which I realised later should was a typo for Bernard Shaw) where all the dining tables are actually old Singer sewing machines, minus the sewing machines...

Tell us where you bought these letters, said the female officer impatiently, looking me straight in the eye. The male officer remained silent and eyed me up and down, beads of sweat and irritation forming on his upper lip. Israeli men are not known for their patience. I've learnt that much from my boyfriend.

66

Yes, I said, reading his mind. I'm getting to the point. The point we reached, which is also the point where this story should begin, was the little antique shop we discovered after we'd walked down the hill, past the souvenir shops and the old market. It was a shop which sold everything from teddy bears to old radios and cameras, from tins and pens and medical equipment to maps and stools and typewriters and spare parts of old cars and… well, documents and letters.

Do you remember the name of the shop?

I believe it may not even have a name. It's that kind of shop.

And the name of the owner?

I don't really know, but he was a man with greying hair. And he was reading a newspaper.

Can you explain what happened once you entered the shop?

Well, my boyfriend and I looked around for quite some time, without intending to buy anything. It was great, a kind of magical place from the past. Just like playing hide-and-seek with your childhood. Remembering how the dustiest of places were once the most interesting. Losing your sense of time, and… Well, at one point, I noticed this whole pile of documents which looked almost damp, as if they'd been kept in somebody's bathroom for months or something. And that's what made me look at them more closely. And that's what made me notice the handwriting. Which reminded me of something.

You had seen this handwriting before?

Yes, a similar handwriting. Many times.

Where?

In biographies. In museums. In Prague.

What was the reason you decided to buy these documents?

The reason was what the shop owner told me about them. He said he had no idea what they were or what they could mean to anyone. But that some very old woman who smelt bad had come in one day a few weeks before and asked him to hide them. (Hide? he said. I don't hide things. I sell them. I'll be back, she told him. Please hide them for me. Everybody's after these papers. The whole of Tel Aviv. All of Israel. The whole world.)

The owner laughed as he told the story. The old lady looked batty, he continued. Almost a hundred, smelt of urine and cat food gone bad, had no teeth in her mouth and could barely speak. Please, she begged him slowly, as if the very last breath of her very long life may depend on it. Be-va-ka-sha. So he felt sorry for her and pretended to see just how important this was for her. Of course, he told her. I'll hide them for you. Till you come back.

And did the old lady reclaim her papers? asked the female officer, now visibly irritated.

No, she didn't. I was so moved by the story that I asked the shop owner how much he wanted for the papers. He said I could have them for a hundred dollars, as he didn't think the old woman was coming back. I told him he was breaking his promise to a hundred-year-old lady. He took that as haggling and said: Ok, eighty dollars, then. My boyfriend thought I was mad. Which I probably am. You can barely even see anything on those, he cried. Can't you see it's just a bunch of soaking wet, filthy old pages? They weigh a ton, too, he complained, but eventually carried them all the way home. I never carried anything so heavy for any other girl, he said, when we got to the door. Just so you know, beseder?

Later that evening, I carefully detached one sheet from the other. Slowly, carefully, methodically, as if I were peeling skin off an injured patient. It's okay, don't worry, hakol beseder. I know this hurts, but you'll be fine. One, two, three, four. Fifty-four. Ninety-five. I read every single page till the early hours of the morning. Read and cried over every single sentence, sighed over the spread out tentacles of ink, smiled at each and every scrawl. Dried every single word with the help of my hair-dryer. I believe I could write the whole thing out again from memory, the whole ninety-eight pages, if I wanted to. Because…

The male officer finally decided to speak: Because what?

What I mean is… Don't you see? They are not there any more.

What isn't there any more?

The male officer finally opened the suitcase, which had been closed throughout the questioning. He wanted to make sure the sheets were still there, and seemed relieved to discover they were.

What are you saying? What is not there any more?

The words, of course. Each time I used the hairdryer, the words disappeared. It is just the greetings you can read now. Lieber Franz. Lieber Max. Alles Gute. Greetings and endings, that's all.

The female officer's eyes became as big and round as falafels.

But– she began, picking up one of the sheets. And she stopped. She just couldn't let it come out, whatever it was she wanted to say. Which probably was Follow Me.

So you see, dear Franz, I could read your soul. All they could see was ninety-eight blank sheets of paper. Don't worry. Your secret is safe with me.

.

KAFKAESQUE

The man said: Let me tell you this. I am the reincarnation of Franz Kafka.

I believed him because his ears were pointed and his voice was melancholy. Everybody in the café turned round to look at him and he went on saying the same thing over and over, gesticulating dramatically, pointing at people inside or outside the café, repeating: Let me tell you this; let me tell you this.

There was something about him – his sad eyes, his crazy voice, his pointed ears – which drew me to him. Something of myself I saw in him, maybe. I don't know. The mad aura, the wildness, the look of the starving artist. The point is, we were soon sitting at the same table, sharing the same bottle of bad red wine. He was talking; I was listening. I let him tell me anything he wanted, without interrupting him much, except to fill up his glass – nodding in the right places, or just adding one word here, two words there. The truth is, the life he was relating to me, real or imagined, sounded much more interesting than mine.

And then he started confiding in me. Let me tell you this, there is nothing I did right in life, nothing at all. All my life wasted, gone, all gone. Missed opportunities, wrong roads taken, too many bad decisions made that unmade me. A bitter and twisted wife, long gone and disappeared, was a young woman I loved. Two children, long turned adult, married, divorced, and gone to live with their dreams in the dark. So here I am now – just me, my pale old face, my white hair, my hat and my long black overcoat. Just me and the sad story of my life. Nobody knows me or cares about me or looks at me except when I say that I am the reincarnation of Franz Kafka. So call me impersonator, impostor, fucking loser, but let me tell you this. I once met him.

Met? Who?

Franz. Franz Kafka.

You've met Franz Kafka?

Yes, on Charles Bridge. In the beginning it was a pleasure to meet him. But it ended badly – the story of my life. Was a pleasure, Franz, said. I really enjoy your books, the one about the man-cockroach-man and the one about Josef K. the guilty-not-guilty. All those convoluted ideas, sentences and descriptions of back streets and people running away from others and themselves. It's been a real pleasure to meet you, Franz; thank you for your time – oh, and could you please sign this for me? I took a copy of the *Letter to His Father* out of my pocket. I'd read it so many times that it had gone yellow at the edges, the ink had almost faded. And do you know what? He just gave me a look of disdain and said: If I'd known some schmuck like you was going to read my books I'd never have written them. Can you believe it? Kafka called me a schmuck. So what was I supposed to do? I lunged at him and held him by the neck and shook him, and my anger got the better of me, so I just shook and shook him, shouting: Who do you think you are, you – you son-of-a – Just who are you calling a schmuck? Who do you think is the schmuck around here? He turned white – whiter than before – and I couldn't tell you exactly when it happened, but—

But what?

I killed him.

You killed Franz Kafka?

Well, yes. Or if you like, I caused his death. Accidentally.

What do you mean?

I threw him over the bridge. And I just stood there while he called for help, I just stood there and watched, while my son was swept further and further by the current, until all I could see was a white, ghostly figure – my little boy going back in time, drowning, swallowing his pride, being swallowed up, up and down his little body, up and down, down, down, and I just stood and stared, and he stared back with all the hatred, the terrible fear I had thrown into his face all his life, with all the anger I had thrown over the bridge together with him. I hate you, he was shouting from underneath the water. I hate you, you bastard! I'll hate you till the day I die. And that's what happened. He hated me till the day he died. He called me a schmuck and he was right.

But let me tell you this: I loved my son. I just didn't know how to cross the river between us. That's all. I just didn't know how to build bridges. I'll write all this down one day on a piece of paper which I'll burn, together with all the anger and guilt I carry in my heart. Then, I'll scatter my ashes over a bridge.

NOT ETGAR KERET

"We laughed so much we cried," they said.

The funniest guy ever, they said. You missed a great film, and watching it on DVD will only add to your misery. You missed the chance of a lifetime to visually assess his wife, to admire him, her, him, even from a distance. You could have felt his creative energy go straight to your soul as you shook hands. You could have smiled at him. You could have said: "I'm so happy to be able to tell you this face to face, Etgar: I love you. Oh God, I love you."

You got the date wrong? they stared at me, aghast. Jesus, you miss a bus. You miss a train. Hell, you may even miss a flight! But no one. Ever. Misses. Etgar. Keret.

So, he came to my home town, talked about his life, screened a film he directed with his wife and left, before I got the chance to even hear his last words to the packed audience – which probably were: "Thank you, thank you, really, truly. I am touched there were so many of you here this evening. I am touched that I have touched you. Your lives will never be the same again."

And then he signed books and drew odd little pictures in them with his left hand. And he smiled, kind of, and grinned, kind of, and he shook hands, and he smiled some more. Drank a glass of red wine, spilt a little on the floor, stepped on it, talked to a few people, looked at his watch. And left.

My body felt like a missing person for weeks. A limp, transparent, lump of nothingness, jellyfished by my own stupidity. (What does jellyfished mean? It means Don't Cry for Me Argentina, it means fuck the calendar, it means there's a bee inside your head that wants to escape, it means really, truly, you can't even read dates, it means you never got a chance, it means you should go and crack a few walnuts with your teeth, it means say something ugly like Krankenstein a few thousand times, smash a

73

few white plates against white walls, kick yourself or ask someone to do it for you, it means a whole load of useless things, pick and choose, two for the price of one, are you happy now?)

Even the supermarket cashier who's known me for six years (give or take) gave me a sad look and asked, almost apologetically, if I was all right. "Of course I am," I said, picking up the bag of unripe avocadoes and dropping it back into the trolley, "What makes you ask?" "I dunno," she said. "You look – different. Kind of – er… lost." I've always thought unripe avocadoes look and feel like old-fashioned hand grenades. Hard and green.

And suddenly I felt I was a character in a story who had only seven or eight minutes to tell the world the story of her life in a monologue, or a rant. "Lost?" I cried. "You think I look lost? I'm not crossing borders and you're not an immigration officer in a fucking airport! I'm buying avocadoes for Christ's sake! What do you care what I look like? But just think, there could be a reason for the way somebody looks. There's a reason for everything. Straighten your back and look around you. We're all in our own little world here, we're all a little lost, we're all hiding something, we've all missed out on something, we're all fucked, right? Spot the ghastly women with the tattooed eyebrows and breast implants whose husbands are screwing East Europeans, spot the schoolgirl who's two months pregnant and hiding it under a loose T-shirt, spot the gum-chewing bald-headed sonofabitch who screwed his best friend's girlfriend last night, spot the bureaucrat and his pickled smile, fat wallet and cancerous cells, the hooligan with crazy, curly hair. Now spot the difference between them and you. And now let me tell you why I look lost. I've missed something."

"That'll be 9 Euros and 86 cents," she replied calmly. Maybe she hadn't heard me.

In the Lost and Found Department at Larnaca Airport they once found the suitcase of a great author. He'd been in such a hurry to leave the island, he left his luggage behind. After it had started gathering dust there for weeks and nobody had claimed it, my friend Nick who is a baggage handler called me to ask if I'd like him to open it slightly and take a peek. "Yes, take a peek," I said, "but call me while you're doing it. I want to be there, too."

One cold Wednesday night in mid-January, my mobile rang, and half-dressed, half-undressed, I answered it. "Are you ready?" said Nick. "I can't do this any other time. There's nobody around. It's our only chance." I told him to be quick about it. He said he had to find a way to break the lock. "Try 1967 before you do," I yawned. It worked. "Ok!" I could hear the excitement in his breath, as he lowered the suitcase on the cold ground, slooooowly started separating the top half from the bottom half like a kind of surgeon and ... Nick went silent. Suddenly very silent. "Come on!" I cried, "Tell me what you see. The suspense is killing me..." In the fifty-five seconds which followed I expected him to say something like: "Oh, how boring! Shaving kit, boxer shorts, two long-sleeved white shirts, a brown jumper, a pair of jeans, some tea bags, a couple of flyers with stuff written in Hebrew, a T-shirt with a Teddy Bear on it which says 'Every Story has an End'. And some marbles." Instead, Nick said: "You won't believe this." And went quiet. "What?" I yelled. "Won't believe what? Are you finally gonna tell me what you can see?"

"I can see a jellyfish," said Nick. "I think it's dead."

That night, Etgar Keret appeared to me in a dream. At least, he looked like Etgar Keret, so I told him about the suitcase, the dead jellyfish, its shrivelled up body and tentacles, and started crying. "Please don't cry," he said, and hugged me. "Women who cry make me uncomfortable. Do not leave your life unattended. Do not waste your tears. And in any case, I am not Etgar Keret."

Before I could ask who he was, he replied. "I am your car mechanic. Don't you recognise me?"

Now he mentioned it, it finally clicked. I realised after all these years who Stelios, my car mechanic, reminds me of. Same greying, tousled hair, same goofy teeth, same thick lips, same hooked nose, big, brown, downward slanting eyes and upward shooting eyebrows. Same way of appearing out of nowhere, wearing a leather jacket. "I don't know anything about jellyfish," he said. "But let's take a look at your car." He smiled, kind of. And grinned, with all the whiteness of his teeth, while he opened the bonnet with great élan, using his left hand. It was as if he was opening up the way to all kinds of possibilities. A full service of my car and great possibilities. "Come back at three. To pick up your car. It'll be as good as new."

When I woke up, I wondered if the dream had a hidden meaning. Had I checked the oil? Did the brakes work? And the gearbox? The headlights? Because the brakes kind of whistled sometimes and I had no idea what that meant, and no idea what I'd do if my car broke down in a deserted part of town. Or maybe the car in the dream was symbolic of my heart, or something.

Lately, I've been trying to do with people and events in my life what I do with words, sentences and whole documents in front of a computer screen. Delete, edit, discard, drag to and remove from Recycle Bin. The writer in me thinks it is bound to have a therapeutic effect, all this deleting, blanking, blotting out the person or thing I'd rather not remember. It doesn't always work. In fact, it has the opposite effect. The more I try to delete or forget, the more I remember, the more I want them to shut up, the more the characters talk.

A friend told me a long time ago it has only snowed once in Tel Aviv in the past sixty years. It was his father's third birthday. His parents took him up to the top of the roof of their house, a little boy dressed in a fur coat, like a cute teddy bear. He showed me a photo of him, them, all huddled up in that whiteness, somewhere in the heart of Tel Aviv. "It's hard to make out the faces in a black-and-white photograph," he said, "with all that snow falling."

I want to end this story with another story which ended some time ago. This is like the final scene in a film. It's kind of bittersweet. And, actually, it hasn't got much to do with Etgar Keret – except that the two people in it recommended Keret stories to each other, once upon a time. It's a scene I play over and over in my head, without ever managing to edit or change anything at all.

There are two people, a man and a woman, on a rooftop in Tel Aviv. It's snowing for the first time in centuries, and the man asks the woman how she's doing. Before she can open her mouth he asks her: "Do you remember that night I got stung by a jellyfish?" She smiles and nods. She remembers it more clearly than anything in her life. It stings. No words come out of her mouth. Then he says: "Do you miss me?" She smiles again, but again, not a single word comes out. Her voice is cold, shivering, hiding. And before his voice disappears completely: "Meet me in Cafeneto at Dizengoff Centre at three?" She knows there is no answer. That neither of them has any way of moving or getting there. Because it was all such a long time ago.

At the end of the story the two characters are trapped in a snow globe, and some unknown hand shakes it and turns it upside down, forever and ever. The snow falls into her eyes and everywhere, stings her bare skin, because she's dressed in a cotton summer dress and because it's July and because all the quotation marks start falling, too, just like the snow, and who knows who said what and when and why, because everything finally makes perfect sense or no sense at all, just like in a dream.

And now let me tell you why I look lost. I've missed something. I am touched that I have touched you. Your life will never be the same again. Do not leave your life unattended. Do not waste your tears. We laughed so much, we cried. And, in any case, I am not Etgar Keret.

"It's so green here," says the dead man. "I can play the violin for as long as I want. Nobody complains."

His wife cries into the refrigerator, looks for the tomatoes which ripened days before he died. The fridge is full, her life empty, and hanging in the air, the sobs of the people at the funeral. Their sighs – and the tears, and her tears.

"I've been invited to a wedding," the dead man says, "And I want you to know that I've decided to give up smoking."

Every day, there are messages on the phone, hundreds of them. Once or twice, he just clears his throat, and she waits. But then there is nothing: just twenty seconds of blank.

When there are no messages, loneliness scratches her face and punches the inside of her mouth. That's when she enters the museum of memories, disappears deep inside it, looking at all the exhibits carefully before moving onto the next, and next, and next one. Following the echoes of his heartbeat to an underground place she never knew existed.

Once, she found the small chicken bone he almost choked on, years ago, at their daughter's wedding. Another time, the smell of his aftershave packed inside a violin case. A never-worn tuxedo.

Time passes, she crosses out the days. In the supermarket queue one day, a friend she hasn't seen for months asks after her husband. "He's fine," she replies. "He's as happy as a baby."

"I'm watching the sunset," he says. "And drinking ice tea."

And then, weeks later, he decides to tell her about the girl. The one who cried most at his funeral, hiding her face behind huge dark glasses, fitting her awkward body into the crowd. Her chain-smoking hands deep in the pockets of her black coat – fidgeting, shaking, nervous.

"I loved her," he says. "She was the love of my life."

It is not true. I'm imagining things. I need to snap out of this.

In the museum of memories, she throws things, picks them up, and throws them at the walls again. Unplugs the answering machine, looks at herself in the mirror, looks at the answering machine, dusts, arranges, rearranges and starts kicking everything she knows in the ribs.

"I would travel the universe to find her again."

It isn't true. I'm not listening. Nothing he says will ever make sense again. Nothing.

MAPLESS

Maria woke up one morning and could not remember where she was. She tried to look it up, to use a GPS. Nothing was happening. She called people and asked them if they knew where they were. They said they did. She tried to remember what her country was called, what street she lived on, which floor. It seemed important for a while, to remember all that information because it was the kind of information you needed to fill in application forms, to prove to people who you were.

When she decided to leave her house for a while, she had no idea which road to take. Everything looked the same and yet different. The houses all seemed to be there but they looked flimsy, as if made of paper. She had to make her own way without a map, like a sleepwalker in a city of snoring people. Not even a compass in her head, nothing. She needed something like a bookmark, something to latch onto, except that she wasn't reading a book, didn't need to remember where she'd finished reading, which sentence, which word. She needed to find the right place in the real world.

She reached for her mobile phone but it was out of battery and she had no idea where she'd left the charger. Perhaps if she carried on walking a little, things would start falling into place.

Everything around her was blue, green and brown. She could tear it up, and put it back together differently, a different map of the world, a different universe. I'm not sure about this at all, she thought. Not sure about the universe, or how to remain there.

She considered the times she'd had to wait for people and the times people had had to wait for her, for flights, buses. "All our life is a clockwork and a ridiculous sticking to times, schedules and other such things," she thought. She was suddenly a mapless person, and could make no sense of anything at all. The sky was blue and that was just about the only thing she was sure about.

She decided to join a queue of tired-looking people who seemed to be buying tickets for something. In the queue an Englishman laughed as he told the anecdote about the little old Greek woman who'd made her way to the cashpoint of the supermarket by jumping the queue. The Greeks have no idea what a queue is, said the Englishman. They don't see the point. Not like us Brits, we're forever queuing up for all kinds of reasons, to talk to someone at a desk, at the till, at the bank, at the post office, at the airport. People behind us pushing and shoving, and in front of us silently shuffling their feet or answering their mobile phone. We can tell them: please join the queue, it's the respectable thing to do in this country. A queue is a kind of road that people make, to get to a place which is not that far away.

"Well, at least I know where I'm going now," Maria muttered, getting closer to the ticket counter. "But is it really where I want to be?"

She left the queue in panic and walked along different roads and streets and tree lined boulevards whose names she tried to guess. Freud Boulevard. Relativity Street. Happiness Road. And then her phone started ringing (or was it her imagination?)and a familiar male voice at the other end asked: "Hey darling, are you all right? I've been trying to reach you for about an hour. Where are you?" "I'm out walking," she replied, and felt that she was telling him the truth. "Meet me at Dino's for lunch?" the reassured male voice asked. "Of course," she replied.

Eventually she found herself in a park, sat on a bench and watched some children playing on the swings and see-saws. They were laughing. She asked one of them if she knew where she lived. "I think you turn right and then left and then right again and you get there. It's a house. You can ask my mum."

Maria nodded and looked into the distance.

SELFIE

The receptionist was tired of giving directions and saying the same things over and over. She circled the streets on the map with her blue pen and handed the leaflet to the man. It was late afternoon. She tried to smile. The man pointed at the map and said something in a language the receptionist had never heard before, a sentence which ended with the word "bone china". In the next sentence, addressed to the woman next to him, he included the words "porcelain" and "cloisonné". The woman, a blonde in an off-white summer dress and navy blue peep-toe shoes, leaned towards him to take a closer look at the brochure. As she did so, his right arm touched her left. They seemed united in their own language and in their quest for objects of fragile beauty.

Selfie with toast. The receptionist's one bedroom apartment is full of clutter and shoes. She dusts cushions from her 9th floor balcony into sunlight. There is no wind today, no air. Today, on her day off, she sits at the kitchen table drinking coffee, eating toast. Once, a long time ago, she wanted to become a different woman every day, because she wanted to surprise men. Now she takes selfies at every opportunity, sees herself as a different woman in each one, as different as the setting will allow. She does not need permission to be who she wants, to be infinitely different to who she was yesterday, or to lose the plot.

As she approaches the end of her novel (257th page) she knows that there is not a lot that is fictional in her book. It's all about people she meets at the reception desk. Those people are as real to her as the characters in her book: the beautiful people who check in, excited at the prospect of exploring a new city, of surprising each other in bed, the handsome men who check out with their neatly packed belongings in expensive suitcases and order taxis to the airport. It was exciting, for a while. She counted beads of sweat on men's upper lips, trying to decide whether the women next to them were their wives or mistresses, princesses or sluts. She went home and wrote pages and pages.

Nothing really surprised the receptionist anymore. Not a lot, anyway. Sometimes she tried to imagine the contents of the suitcases they left at her desk while they paid for their stay. A flag, a pipe, a mobile charger, a 100-dollar bill, a whip, a tea set, a semen-stained bra, a condom, a tailor made suit, a silk scarf…Things that would soon be unpacked, discarded, or washed, ironed and hung, or hidden in wardrobes large enough for two children to play hide and seek. They failed to shock the older her, the one who'd been packing her own suitcase for many years, preparing for that long trip away from reality, any day now, as soon as she put the final touches, added the last words, to her manuscript. They were some of the things which had made her who she was, these strange, forgotten, used, broken objects. The heroine in the latest chapter carried seaweed and shells and clams home. The chapter ended with her snorkelling with clown fish, laughing (with difficulty) underwater. The one before wore a chador and told stories with her eyes, unbelievably long and erotic stories that her body could not. The young woman in the orange miniskirt made her tongue bleed by kissing the Star of David on the man's chest. "There are still some secrets on the tip of my tongue," she said. She pronounced "tongue" as "tong", giving the impression that her first language may be French.

Selfie in Cellophane. A man saved the receptionist's life with the love he gave her. His presence in this story is not indispensable, yet necessary, in order to show that there was once love. She keeps the memories she has of him, some in aluminium foil, some in cellophane. Her legs wrapped round his body, in clingfilm. It was her way of telling him she never wanted him to leave. His lips covered with a piece of aluminium foil. The mole on his neck, her melting heart.

Once, they went together to a bazaar. Her yellow sandals got covered in dust as they passed by deft-witted shopkeepers, one stall owner following them along the street, offering to reduce the price, saying he had other goods, handbags, beaded dresses, robes, all beautiful workmanship, all cheap bargains. "That funny little shape you make with your mouth when you're just about to start bargaining kills me," her boyfriend said, and her eyes glittered with drama, or maybe it's just a trick of the camera in that particular photo where they're smiling together. Maybe, even in that photo, behind that wide smile, she was afraid, like all women, that love would not keep that well.

The cloisonné couple greeted her the next morning on their way out. Her dress was salmon pink, her shoes black. His linen suit immaculate. The breakfast room was half-empty: three older couples and a group of Germans. The youngest porter was explaining something to a taxi driver, something that the taxi driver refused to understand. There was a smell of bacon and hot tea, and outside, humidity hung in the air like unshed tears. Commuters were going to work, all seemingly following the same route, all solemnly following one another: businessmen, dealers, bankers, financiers, managers, lawyers who knew their daily routine by heart and googled things that might come in handy one day. Persian carpets, blue Delft porcelain, Turkish Lira, Elgin marbles, winding staircases, especially winding staircases, which you could climb in haste, to get to your superiority complex. The cloisonné woman buys a hand-painted tea set as beautiful as it is frightening. Frightening because it might break, beautiful because it will never age. She might break too, one day, when she finds she is aging. For now, she is pleased, and he behind her, pleased with her pleasure puts one arm around her waist and holds her. She smiles like Mona Lisa, an ambiguous smile on an indeterminate face, clinging to a knowledge which could raise eyebrows.

Selfie with peep-toe shoes and rice. The receptionist is writing the last page of this chapter and has become the blonde in Room 565. She is the blonde in the salmon pink dress who goes to the bathroom in terrible pain, kneels on the floor, presses her forehead on the cold tiles and is violently sick. She could be pregnant, or she could be dying. The author will decide later. "It's something I ate," she groans between the spasms. "Must be something I ate." The fresh soap and towels of the hotel room do nothing to stop her remembering the heavy smell of the incense in the last shop where they stopped.

They had later gone to dine at the restaurant the receptionist had recommended, and bowls of steaming rice and dishes of spicy food had been placed before them. The incense still swirled round her nostrils. He had heaped his plate until it was swimming with brightly coloured vegetables in a yellow sauce. A full glass of white wine stood by his plate. "It's great!" he repeated over and over. "I don't know what it is… but it's delicious." As he spoke, he spat a grain of rice on the tablecloth. His mouth opened and shut and he said things to her which she no longer understood. Yes, she nodded. Oh no, she said. And one more word: absolutely. Which meant absolutely nothing. She felt as if she were on auto-pilot.

Her stomach is empty now, her glazed face finally broken, her blue peep-toe shoes stained with vomit. "I'm fine," she says when he asks her. She always says she's fine when people ask her. There is a neon light sign on a side street somewhere not far from their hotel. It says "I'm fine", and flashes on and off, twenty-four hours a day.

CECI N'EST PAS UNE PIPE

I suppose the story must start, not with a pipe, as its title suggests, but with a menu. The menu of a Greek tavern which specialises in serving meze, with a twist. Except that you don't know that until you've read the menu. Not the English or German or Russian menu, but the authentic Greek one. That's where all the rude words are.

She laughs, of course, when she sees what's on offer. All at quite reasonable prices, service included. "Perverted Salad" at five euros (which is actually 2.93 Cyprus Pounds, for those still living in the past). Various parts of male anatomy, grilled. Twelve euros. Does one keep a straight face while placing the order? (Medium rare please, with chips. Well done please, with rice). And she forgets all about food, or that she was hungry in the first place. She blushes and laughs at the same time. Or maybe she just blushes.

"Yes, there are a few rude words on the Greek menu," she explains, to her English friend who is visiting for a week. "How did you know?"

"I read about this place in the in-flight magazine. Highly recommended. It said, just make sure you take a Cypriot along with you, so she can translate the Greek menu. Supposed to be really raunchy. So, will you?"

"Will I? What?"

"Translate."

The Englishman asks for a menu in Greek. This is where Magritte's pipe comes in, because on the outside it looks like an English menu but it isn't. And yet it is a menu. The man is English, speaks perfect English, looks English. And yet he asks for the Greek one. Ceci n'est pas un menu grec.

"Excuse me…"

"Yes?"

"Could I please…"

"Yes?"

"…have the Greek menu?"

Yes, the waitress is sure he has asked for the Greek menu, and so she places it on the table a little cautiously, and disappears into the kitchen.

"Thank you," he says.

"For what?"

"For translating so well. Now I know exactly what I'd like to order."

"Really?"

"Definitely. Nipples in red wine sauce. And you?"

"Mmmm. Not sure. Maybe, er, the, er, sausage in the yoghurt sauce."

"That's not the word they used on the menu, though, is it?"

"Well, no, I suppose not."

"So why don't you say it?"

"Say what?"

"The real word. What you really want to eat."

She laughs again. And blushes, and laughs, and blushes and hopes the waitress is not listening in on this conversation.

But, of course, the waitress is. She wonders why the man is laughing and the woman is blushing, or the woman is laughing and the man is not. They are just any other couple, but there is something strange about them. Almost as if they can communicate without even talking. Because they're not even talking. Ceci n'est pas une conversation.

"And if I were to write a story about this," the waitress thinks… Because that's what she does on her nights off. She loves making up little stories about the couples she sees eating at these tables. Different faces every night. Snippets of conversation. Laughter. Whispers and holding hands. Stained napkins. The noise that cutlery makes on crockery. The lightness of cigarette smoke.

Sometimes there are whole groups of people, and once, she remembers, there was even a speech. That was when the wine glass was lightly touched with a knife three times, to announce that a speech was about to be made. Lightly touched, but the glass broke, and everyone laughed. She didn't find it funny herself. She took it as a bad sign for whoever the speech was for. "Let me take this opportunity to…" the speaker began, but the waitress was called to another table, so had to miss the beginning of the speech. When they called her later about the broken glass, all she heard was the last five words: "…so sorry to see you go."

"And if I were to write a story about this strange couple," she thinks, "I would begin right here. Beginning a story is easy. It's the endings that are difficult. So how exactly will this story end? If it has a beginning, a middle and an end, where are they? And whose responsibility is it to find them? The reader's? Or the author's?"

The couple is still talking. And not talking. What is left of their meal is cleared away ("One of them doesn't like fetta," thinks the waitress. "Which one?") Now they order Cypriot coffee, both without sugar. "Skettos," says the Englishman, with a totally English accent. "No sugar," says the Cypriot woman, with a totally Cypriot accent. And one of them is still laughing inwardly, but which one? The waitress can hear laughter, even when it's silent. And she thinks: "Oh, so not really a couple at all. Just two people together, and they just happen to be a man and a woman."

In her story she will make them more interesting. They will be lovers in a bizarre situation in a restaurant with a strange Greek menu. They will order the full mezé and pretend the Greek name given to each dish has rude connotations. They will laugh at the rude words on their plates and in their mouths. Nobody else will know what they're laughing at. Not even the waitress. At times they will converse in fluent Greek, at others in fluent English, not a trace of an accent on either part. The woman will be blonde and the man dark, or vice versa. Nobody will really know why they are here, or what they are discussing. Nobody will really know whether their story has ended or just begun. Nobody will really know whether it is a story at all.

ABOUT THE AUTHOR

Nora Nadjarian lives in Nicosia, Cyprus. She has published three collections of poetry: *The Voice at the Top of the Stairs* (2001), *Cleft in Twain* (2003) and *25 Ways to Kiss a Man* (2004). Her second poetry collection *Cleft in Twain* was cited by *The Guardian* in an article on the literature of the new European Union member states in 2004.

In addition to a book of short stories, *Ledra Street* (2006) and a book of fairy-tale inspired microfiction *Girl, Wolf, Bones* (2011), she has had work published online and in journals in the UK, the United States, Australia and elsewhere. Her stories have won prizes and commendations in the Commonwealth Short Story Competition, the Binnacle International Ultra-Short Competition and the Seán Ó Faoláin Short Story Prize.

ALSO BY NORA NADJARIAN

The Voice at the Top of the Stairs
Cleft in Twain
25 Ways to Kiss a Man
Ledra Street
Girl, Wolf, Bones

Some of the stories in this collection have previously appeared in
*Best European Fiction 2011 (Dalkey Archive
Press), Metazen, blueprintpress, World Literature Today, Kunapipi, Blue Fifth
Review, Liars' League, Southword, Tel Aviv Short Stories (Ang-Lit.
Press), Etchings (Ilura Press), Bookanista, In Our Own Words (Volume 8)*